MAIGRET

HAS

SCRUPLES

MAIGRET HAS SCRUPLES

by Georges Simenon

Translated from the French by
Robert Eglesfield

A Harvest / HBJ Book
A Helen and Kurt Wolff Book
Harcourt Brace Jovanovich, Publishers
San Diego   New York   London

HBJ

Copyright © 1958 by Georges Simenon
Copyright renewed 1986 by Georges Simenon

Requests for permission to make copies
of any part of the work should be mailed to:
Permissions, Harcourt Brace Jovanovich, Publishers,
Orlando, Florida 32887.

Library of Congress Cataloging-in-Publication Data
Simenon, Georges, 1903–
Maigret Has Scruples.
"A Helen and Kurt Wolff book."
Translation of: Les Scruples de Maigret.
I. Title.
ISBN 0-15-655160-8 (Harvest/HBJ : pbk.)

Printed in the United States of America

First Harvest/HBJ edition 1988

A B C D E F G H I J

MAIGRET

HAS

SCRUPLES

1

THIS scarcely happens more than once or twice a year at the Quai des Orfèvres, and sometimes it is over so soon that no one has time to notice it: suddenly, after a period of feverish activity, during which cases follow one after another without a breathing-space, when they are not cropping up three or four at a time, working the whole staff so hard that the inspectors, for want of sleep, end up haggard and red-eyed, suddenly there is a dead calm, a blank, one might say, barely punctuated by a few telephone calls of no importance.

This had been the case the day before, a Monday, it is true, a day which is always slacker than the rest, and at eleven o'clock in the morning this was still the atmosphere on Tuesday. In the vast corridor, there were at most two or three seedy-looking informers, who had come to make their reports and were hanging about uneasily, while in the inspectors' office everyone, except for those who were suffering from influenza, was at his post.

Whereas in an emergency Maigret was generally short-handed and had the utmost difficulty in finding enough men to put on to a case, he could have drawn, today, on almost his entire squad.

It is true that it was the same nearly everywhere in Paris. It was January 10th. People, after the holidays, were living at a slower pace, with a vague hang-over, and the prospect of rent to pay and income-tax returns to make close at hand.

The sky, in keeping with their consciences and their spirits, was a dull grey, more or less the same grey as the pavements. There was a chill in the air, but not enough to be interesting and to be mentioned in the papers, an unpleasant chill, nothing more, which you only noticed after you had been walking in the streets for some time.

The radiators, in the offices, were burning hot, making the atmosphere closer than ever, and from time to time there were gurgling sounds in the pipes, mysterious noises which came from the boiler-room.

Like schoolboys in their classrooms after the examinations, all and sundry were attending to those little jobs which are usually put off until later, finding in their drawers forgotten reports, statistics to be worked out, dreary administrative tasks.

The people who are talked about in the papers were nearly all on the Côte d'Azur or at winter sports.

If Maigret had still been in possession of his stove, which had been left long after the central heating had been installed but which had finally been removed, he would have broken off from time to time to stoke it up, poking the fire so as to produce a rain of red ashes.

He was not feeling out of sorts, but he was not in good form either, and he had wondered for a moment, in the bus bringing him from the Boulevard Richard-Lenoir, whether he might not be sickening for the influenza.

Perhaps it was his wife who was worrying him? The day before, his friend Pardon, the doctor in the Rue Picpus, had telephoned him unexpectedly.

'Hullo, Maigret. . . . Now don't tell Madame Maigret that I've told you about this . . .'

'Told me about what?'

'She has just been to see me and she insisted that I wasn't to speak to you about it. . . .'

It was less than a year since the chief-inspector himself had been to see Pardon and had asked him to say nothing to his wife about his visit.

'Above all, don't go and start worrying. I've examined her carefully. There's nothing seriously wrong. . . .'

Maigret had been as dull-witted, the day before, when he had had this telephone call, as he was this morning, with the same administrative

3

report in front of him, waiting to be put into shape.

'What does she say is the matter with her?'

'For some time now, she has been getting out of breath going upstairs, and her legs feel heavy too, especially in the morning. Nothing to worry about, as I said before. Only, her circulation isn't quite what it ought to be. I've prescribed some tablets for her to take with every meal. I ought to tell you too, so that you won't be taken by surprise, that I've put her on a diet. I should like her to lose ten or twelve pounds, because that would ease the strain on her heart.'

'You are sure that . . .'

'I swear to you there's absolutely no danger at all, but I thought it best to let you know about it. If I were you, I should pretend I hadn't noticed anything. What frightens her most of all is the thought of your worrying about her. . . .'

Knowing his wife, he felt sure that she had gone and bought the prescribed medicine at the first chemist's she had come to. The telephone call had come in the morning. At midday, he had watched Madame Maigret, who had taken no tablets while he was there. In the evening it was the same. He had hunted for a bottle or a pillbox in the sideboard drawers, and then, in a casual way, in the kitchen.

Where could she have hidden her tablets? She had eaten less, and had not taken any dessert, though she usually enjoyed it.

'I think I must start slimming a bit,' she had

said jokingly. 'I'm beginning to burst out of my dresses. . . .'

He had every confidence in Pardon. He was not alarmed. All the same it worried him, or rather, to be more precise, it made him sad.

He had been the first, the year before, with three weeks of complete rest. Now it was his wife's turn. This meant that they had arrived almost imperceptibly at the age of petty tribulations, when minor repairs are necessary, rather like cars which, all of a sudden, need to be sent to the garage nearly every week.

Only, for cars, you can buy spare parts. You can even put in a new engine.

When the porter knocked at his door, which he opened as usual without waiting for an answer, Maigret was not conscious of these thoughts. He raised his head from his file, and looked at old Joseph with big eyes that you might have thought were asleep.

'What is it?'

'Somebody who insists on seeing you personally.'

And Joseph, who made no noise as he walked, put a form on the corner of the desk.

Maigret read a name written in pencil but, as this name meant nothing to him, took no notice of it. Later he would only remember that it was a two-syllabled name, which probably began with an M. Only the Christian name, Xavier, stuck in his memory, because it was that of his first chief at the Quai des Orfèvres, old Xavier Guichard.

Under the printed words: 'Purpose of Call', there was something like: 'Urgently needs to talk to Chief-Inspector Maigret.'

Joseph waited, impassively. It was gloomy enough in the office for the lamps to be lit, but the chief-inspector had not thought of it.

'Will you see him?'

He said yes with a nod of the head, shrugging his shoulders slightly. Why not? The next moment, a visitor of about forty was shown in, whose appearance had nothing special about it and who could have been any one of the thousands of men you see, at six o'clock in the evening, walking hurriedly towards the nearest Metro station.

'I must apologize for troubling you, Chief-Inspector . . .'

'Sit down.'

His visitor was a little nervous, though not inordinately so, overawed rather, like so many others who entered this same office. He was wearing a dark overcoat, which he unbuttoned before sitting down, keeping his hat on his knees at first, then, a little later, putting it by his feet on the carpet.

He smiled then, a mechanical smile, no doubt a sign of timidity. After giving a little cough, he said:

'The hardest thing is getting started, isn't it? Of course, like everybody else, I've repeated to myself I don't know how many times what I was going to say to you, but, now the time has come, it's all getting muddled up. . . .'

6

Another smile, angling for some sign of approval or encouragement from the chief-inspector. But the latter's interest had not been awakened. The man had come at the wrong time, when his mind was asleep.

'You must have lots of calls of this sort, from people who come to talk to you about their little troubles, convinced that they are interesting.'

He was dark, and not bad-looking, although his nose was a little crooked and his lower lip too fleshy.

'I can assure you that that isn't the case with me and that I hesitated a long time before bothering a man as busy as you are.'

He must have expected to find a desk littered with files, with two or three telephones ringing at once, inspectors coming and going, and witnesses or suspects slumped on chairs. That was indeed more or less what he would have found on any other day, but his disappointment failed to amuse the chief-inspector, who looked as if he were thinking of nothing in particular.

In fact, he was looking at his visitor's suit, and thinking that it was made of a good cloth and that it must have been cut by a local tailor. A suit of a grey colour that was almost black. Black shoes. A quiet tie.

'Let me assure you, Chief-Inspector, that I'm not mad. I don't know if you know Dr. Steiner, in the Place Denfert-Rochereau. He's a neurologist, which, I believe, is more or less the same as a psychiatrist, and he has appeared several times as an expert witness in the assize courts.'

Maigret's thick eyebrows rose a little way, but not unduly far.

'You've been to see Steiner?'

'Yes, I went and asked him to examine me, and incidentally I might say that his examinations last a full hour and that he leaves nothing to chance. He found nothing wrong. He regards me as completely normal. As for my wife, whom he hasn't seen . . .'

He stopped, because his monologue was not exactly the one he had prepared, and he tried to remember the precise wording. With a mechanical gesture, he had taken a packet of cigarettes out of his pocket and did not dare to ask permission to smoke.

'You may,' said Maigret.

'Thank you.'

His fingers were somewhat clumsy. He was nervous.

'I beg your pardon. I ought to control myself better than this. I can't help being agitated. This is the first time I've seen you in the flesh, all of a sudden, in your office, with your pipes . . .'

'May I ask what your occupation is?'

'I ought to have begun with that. It isn't a very common occupation and, like so many people, you are probably going to smile. I work at the Grands Magasins du Louvre, in the Rue de Rivoli. My official title is head salesman in the toy department. So you can imagine that in the holiday season I was worked to death. Actually, I have a special job which takes most of my time: you see, I'm in charge of the electric trains.'

It was as if he had forgotten where he was, and why he was there, and was letting himself go on his favourite topic.

'Did you go past the Magasins du Louvre in December?'

Maigret said neither yes nor no. He could not remember. He vaguely recalled a gigantic luminous design, on the façade, but he could not have said what the multicoloured moving figures represented.

'If you did, you must have seen, in the third window on the Rue de Rivoli, an exact reconstruction of Saint-Lazare Station, with all its tracks, its suburban trains and its expresses, its signals, its signal-boxes. It took me three months' work and I had to go to Switzerland and Germany to buy some of the material. It may seem childish to you, but if I told you the amount of money we make on electric trains alone . . . Above all, don't imagine that our customers are just children. There are grown-ups, including men with important positions, who are passionately interested in electric trains, and I'm often called to private residences to . . .'

He broke off again.

'Am I boring you?'

'No.'

'You're listening?'

Maigret nodded. His caller must have been between forty and forty-five years old and wore a broad, flat wedding-ring in red gold, almost the same as the chief-inspector's. He also had a tie-pin representing a railway signal.

'Now I've forgotten what I was saying. Of course, it wasn't to talk to you about electric trains that I came to see you, and I realize that I'm wasting your time. However, it is essential that you should be able to place me, isn't it? That I should tell you too that I live in the Avenue de Châtillon, near the church of Saint-Pierre de Montrouge, in the XIVth *arrondissement*, and that I've been in the same place for eighteen years. No: nineteen . . . Anyhow, it will be nineteen years in March . . . I'm married . . .'

He was upset at not being any clearer, at having too many details to give. One felt that as ideas came to him he considered them carefully, asking himself whether they were important or not, then expressed them or rejected them.

He looked at his watch.

'It's precisely because I'm married . . .'

He smiled apologetically.

'It would be easier if you asked the questions, but you can't do that, because you don't know what it's all about . . .'

Maigret came close to reproaching himself for being so static. It was not his fault. It was something physical. He found it difficult to take an interest in what he was being told and felt sorry that he had allowed Joseph to introduce the caller.

'I'm listening . . .'

He filled a pipe, for something to do, and threw a glance at the window, behind which there was nothing but a pale grey colour. It was like a worn-out back-cloth in some provincial theatre.

10

'Above all I must stress that I'm not making any accusations, Chief-Inspector. I love my wife. We've been married now for fifteen years, Gisèle and I, and we've never really had a quarrel. I talked about her to Dr. Steiner, after he'd examined me, and he looked anxious and said:

' "I'd rather like you to bring your wife along to see me."

'Only, on what pretext can I ask Gisèle to accompany me on a visit to a neurologist? I can't even say for certain that she's mad, because she goes on with her work without anybody complaining about her.

'You see, I'm not very well educated. I'm a ward of the Board of Guardians, and I've had to teach myself. Anything I know, I've learnt out of books, in my spare time.

'I'm interested in everything, not just in electric trains, as you might imagine, and I consider that knowledge is man's most precious possession.

'I must apologize for going on like this. What I wanted to explain was that, when Gisèle began behaving differently towards me, I went to various libraries, among them the Bibliothèque Nationale, to consult works which I couldn't afford to buy. Apart from that, my wife would have been worried if she'd found them at home . . .'

The proof that Maigret was following this speech more or less closely was that he asked:

'Works on psychiatry?'

'Yes. I don't claim to have understood everything. Most of them are written in a language which is too learned for me. All the same I found some books on neuroses and psychoses which made me think. I suppose you know the difference between neuroses and psychoses? I've also made a study of schizophrenia, but I believe, in all conscience, that it doesn't go as far as that . . .'

Maigret thought of his wife, of Pardon, and noticed a little brown mole at the corner of his visitor's mouth.

'If I've not misunderstood you, you suspect your wife of not being in her normal condition?'

The moment had come and the man went rather pale, swallowed his saliva two or three times, and then, looking as if he were choosing his words carefully and weighing their meaning, declared:

'I am convinced that for several months, five or six at least, my wife has been meaning to kill me. That, Chief-Inspector, is why I came to see you personally. I haven't got any positive proof, otherwise I would have begun with that. But I'm ready to give you what evidence I have, which is of two sorts. First of all the moral evidence, the most difficult to set out, as you will understand, because it consists above all of trifles which are not important in themselves, but which taken all together end up by meaning something.

'As for the material clues, there is one piece of evidence, which I've brought here to show you, and which is the most worrying of all . . .'

He opened his overcoat, then his jacket, took his wallet out of his hip-pocket, and extracted from it a fold of paper such as some chemists still use for headache powders.

It was in fact powder that the paper contained, a powder of a dirty white colour.

'I'm leaving this sample with you, so that you can have it analysed. Before coming to see you, I asked for an analysis from a salesman at the Louvre, who is keen on chemistry and has set up a real laboratory at his home. He was quite definite. It is white phosphide. Not phosphorus, as you might imagine, but phosphide, I've checked it in the dictionary. And I didn't just trust to Larousse. I've also looked up some books on chemistry. White phosphide is a practically colourless powder, which is extremely poisonous. They used it in the old days, in infinitesimal doses, as a cure for certain illnesses, and it's precisely because it's so poisonous that they had to give it up.'

He paused for a moment, a little puzzled at having before him a Maigret who remained impassive and apparently distrait.

'My wife doesn't go in for chemistry. She isn't following any course of treatment. She isn't suffering from any of the illnesses for which a doctor might, just possibly, prescribe zinc phosphide. Now, it wasn't just a few grammes that I found at home, but a bottle containing at least fifty grammes. As it happens, I came across it by accident. On the ground floor, I've got a sort of workshop where I work on the models of my displays and where I do a little research into mechanics. It's only a matter of toys, I know, but, as I explained to you, toys represent . . .'

'I know.'

'One day when my wife was out, I knocked a pot of glue over on my workbench. I opened the cupboard where the brooms and cleaning materials are kept. Looking for a detergent, I found, quite by accident, a bottle without a label which struck me as being a curious shape.

'Now, if you link this find with the fact that, in the course of these last few months, I've felt, for the first time in my life, certain pains which I've described to Dr. Steiner . . .'

The telephone started ringing on the desk. Maigret picked up the receiver, and recognized the voice of the Chief of Police Headquarters.

'Is that you, Maigret? Have you a few minutes to spare? I should like you to meet an American criminologist who is in my office and who very much wants to make your acquaintance . . .'

Putting down the receiver, Maigret looked around. There was nothing of a confidential nature lying on the desk. His visitor did not look like a dangerous man.

'Will you excuse me? It's only for a few minutes . . .'

'Of course . . .'

At the door, however, he stopped automatically, came back across the office, and opened, as he usually did, the door of the inspectors' office. But he gave them no special instructions. He did not think of it.

A few moments later he pushed open the baize door of the chief's office. A big, red-haired fellow got up from an armchair and shook him vigorously by the hand, saying in French, with only the slightest trace of a foreign accent:

'It's a great pleasure for me to see you in the flesh, Monsieur Maigret. When you came to my country, I missed you, because I was in San Francisco and you didn't come as far as that. My friend Fred Ward, who met you in New York and accompanied you to Washington, has told me some fascinating things about you.'

The chief motioned to Maigret to sit down.

'I hope that I'm not disturbing you right in the middle of one of those interrogations that seem so quaint to us Americans?'

The chief-inspector reassured him. The chief's guest offered him a cigarette, then changed his mind.

'I was forgetting that you're a devotee of the pipe . . .'

This happened periodically and there were always the same remarks, the same questions, the same exaggerated and embarrassing admiration. Maigret, who loathed being examined as if he were a freak, used to put a brave face on things and, at these times, he had a special smile which greatly amused his chief.

One question led to another. After talking of technical matters, they recalled some famous cases, on which he was obliged to give his own opinion.

Inevitably, mention was made of his methods, something which always annoyed him because, as he kept repeating without succeeding in destroying the legends, he had never had any methods.

To release him, the chief got up, saying:

'And now, if you would like to come upstairs and see our museum . . .'

This formed part of every visit of this sort and Maigret, after having his hand crushed once more in a clasp stronger than his own, was able to go back to his office.

He stopped short, surprised, on the threshold, for there was no longer anybody in the armchair he had offered his electric-train salesman. The office was empty, with just some cigarette smoke floating about half-way up to the ceiling.

He made for the inspectors' office.

'Has he gone?'

'Who?'

Janvier and Lucas were playing cards, something they did not do as often as three times a year, except when they were on duty all night.

'Never mind . . . It doesn't matter. . . .'

He went into the corridor, where old Joseph was reading the paper.

'So my customer's gone, has he?'

'Not long since. He came out of your office and told me he couldn't wait any longer, and he just had to get back to the shop, where they were waiting for him. Should I have . . . ?'

'No. It doesn't matter.'

The man was free to go, since nobody had asked him to come. It was just then that Maigret realized that he had forgotten his name.

'I suppose, Joseph, that you don't know what he was called either?'

'I must admit, Chief-Inspector, that I didn't look at his form.'

Maigret went back to his room, sat down again, and immersed himself once more in his report, which was anything but exciting. Anyone would have thought that the boiler-room had got out of control, for the radiators had never been so hot and alarming noises could be heard. He nearly got up to turn the control lever, did not feel equal to it, and stretched his hand out towards the telephone.

He meant to ring up the Magasins du Louvre and inquire about the head of the toy department. But, if he did so, wouldn't they wonder why the police were suddenly taking an interest in one of the staff? Wasn't Maigret running the risk of doing his caller a disservice?

He did a little more work, then picked up the receiver almost automatically.

'Will you try to get me a certain Dr. Steiner, who lives in the Place Denfert-Rochereau?'

Less than two minutes later, the telephone rang.

'You are through to Dr. Steiner.'

'Forgive me for troubling you, Doctor . . . This is Maigret speaking . . . The chief-inspector at Police Headquarters, yes . . . I believe you have had a patient recently whose Christian name is Xavier and whose surname escapes me . . .'

The doctor, at the other end of the line, did not appear to remember.

'His job is selling toys . . . Particularly electric trains . . . He apparently went to see you to make sure that he wasn't mad and, after that, he spoke to you about his wife . . .'

'Just a moment, please. I shall have to consult my records.'

Maigret could hear him saying to somebody:

'Mademoiselle Berthe, will you be so kind as to . . .'

He must have moved away from the telephone, for there was nothing more to be heard and the silence lasted for quite a time, so long in fact that Maigret thought that he had been cut off.

Judging by his voice, Steiner was a cold man, probably conceited, conscious, in any case, of his own importance.

'May I ask, Chief-Inspector, why you have rung me up?'

'Because this man was in my office just now and went off before our conversation had finished. Now it so happens that, while I was listening to him, I tore the form on which he'd written his name into little pieces.'

'Had you asked him to come and see you?'
'No.'
'What is he suspected of?'
'Nothing. He came of his own accord to tell me his story.'

'Has something happened?'

'I don't think so. He spoke to me about certain fears which, I believe, he has mentioned to you . . .'

There is scarcely one doctor in a hundred who is as unco-operative as this, and Maigret had happened on that one.

'You know, I suppose,' said Steiner, 'that my professional oath prevents me from . . .'

'I'm not asking you, Doctor, to break your oath. I'm asking you, first of all, for the surname of this Xavier. I can find it out straight away by telephoning the Grands Magasins du Louvre, where he works, but I thought that if I did that I should risk harming him in the eyes of his superiors.'

'Yes, that seems quite likely.'

'I know too that he lives in the Avenue de Châtillon, and my men, by questioning the concierges, would get the same result. In that way, too, we might harm your patient by stirring up gossip.'

'I understand.'

'Well?'

'He's called Marton, Xavier Marton,' said the neurologist, reluctantly.

'When did he go and see you?'

'I think that I can answer that question too. It was about three weeks ago, the twenty-first of December to be precise . . .'

'In other words, just when he was at his busiest with the Christmas rush. I suppose that he was in an excited condition?'

'I beg your pardon?'

'Listen, Doctor, let me tell you once again, I'm not asking you to betray any secrets. We have, as you know, expeditious ways of getting information.'

Silence at the other end of the line, and Maigret could have sworn that it was a disapproving silence. Dr. Steiner clearly had no liking for the police.

'Xavier Marton, since Marton is his name,' Maigret went on, 'behaved like a normal man in my office. However . . .'

The doctor repeated:

'However?'

'I'm not a psychiatrist and, after listening to him, I should like to know whether I've been dealing with an unbalanced character or whether . . .'

'What do you mean by unbalanced?'

Maigret was red in the face and was holding the receiver in a clenched and threatening hand.

'If you have certain responsibilities, Doctor, and if you are pledged to maintain a professional secrecy which I am not trying in any way to make you infringe, we have certain responsibilities too. I don't like to think that I let a man go who, tomorrow, might . . .'

'I let him walk out of my office too.'

'So you don't think that he's mad?'

Another silence.

'What do you think of what he told you about his wife? Here, he didn't have time to get to the end of his story . . .'

'I haven't examined his wife.'

'And from what he told you, you've no idea of . . .'

'No idea.'

'You've nothing to add?'

'Nothing, I'm afraid. Will you excuse me? I have someone here who's getting impatient.'

Maigret hung up as if he would have liked to break the receiver over the doctor's head.

Then, almost immediately, his anger subsided and he shrugged his shoulders, even smiling after a while.

'Janvier!' he shouted, so as to be heard in the next room.

'Yes, Chief.'

'You're to go to the Grands Magasins du Louvre and go up to the toy department. Try to look like a customer. And look for a man who should be the head of the department, between forty and forty-five years old, dark-haired, with a hairy mole to the left of his mouth.'

'What do I ask him?'

'Nothing. If the head of the department answers to that description, then his name is Xavier Marton and that's all that I want to know. Though, while you're there, you might show an interest in electric trains so as to get him to talk. Have a good look at him. That's all.'

'Was it about him you were talking on the phone just now?'

'Yes. You heard all that, did you?'

'You want to know whether he's mad?'

Maigret just shrugged his shoulders. Any other day he would probably not have given more than a few minutes' attention to Marton's call. At Police Headquarters, they are used to visits from lunatics and semi-lunatics, cranks, inventors, males and females who consider themselves marked out to save the world from perdition and others who are convinced that mysterious enemies have designs on their lives or their secrets.

The Special Squad, or the Criminal Squad as it is usually called, is not a mental hospital and, if it deals with these people, it is generally only when they end up by breaking the law, something which, luckily, does not happen straight away.

It was getting on for midday. He thought of telephoning Pardon, but told himself that it was not worth the trouble, that there was nothing in this morning's call more worrying than in a hundred other calls of the same sort that he had had.

Why did he think of the pills his wife had to take with every meal? Because of the zinc phosphide which Xavier Marton claimed to have found in the broom cupboard. Where did Madame Maigret, for her part, hide her pills, so as not to worry her husband?

Intrigued, he resolved to hunt everywhere. She must have thought about it for a long time, and found an artful hiding-place where he would never think of looking.

Well, they would see. In the meantime, he

closed his file, and turned the radiator half-off at last, preferring not to leave the window open during the lunch hour.

Just as he was going out, he noticed the packet of white powder on his desk and took it to Lucas.

'Send that to the laboratory. Tell them to let me know what it is this afternoon.'

On the embankment, the cold took him by surprise and he turned up the collar of his overcoat, plunged his hands into his pockets and made for the bus stop.

He did not like Dr. Steiner at all, and it was about him that he thought much more than about the specialist in electric trains.

2

As on every day for years past, he had no need to knock at the door, which opened just as he was stepping on the mat, and he could not remember ever having used the electric bell.

'You're back early,' remarked his wife.

And, straight away, she frowned imperceptibly, as she did when she saw that he was preoccupied. She never failed in this either. She noticed the slightest change in his mood and, if she did not ask him any outright questions, she none the less tried to guess what was worrying him.

Now, for the moment, it was not the visit of the electric-train man. He might have thought about that on the bus, but what had just given him a serious expression, indeed a rather melancholy look, was a memory which had come to the surface while he was pausing on the second-floor landing. The previous winter, the old

24

woman who lived in the flat above theirs had said to him, when he passed her in front of the concierge's lodge and touched his hat to her:

'You ought to see a doctor, Monsieur Maigret.'

'You think I look ill?'

'No. I hadn't even looked. It's the way you come upstairs. For some time, you've been treading more heavily and, every four or five steps, I can hear you hesitating.'

It was not because of her that he had gone to see Pardon some weeks later, but she was right for all that. How could he explain to his wife that it was because of that memory that his thoughts appeared to be a long way off?

She had not yet laid the table. As usual, he roamed round the dining-room and the sitting-room and, almost unconsciously, began opening drawers, lifting the lid of the sewing-box, and of a red lacquer casket in which they kept odds and ends.

'Are you looking for something?'

'No.'

He was looking for the pills. It intrigued him. He wondered if he would end up by finding the hiding-place.

And then, after all, it was true that he had none of his usual go. Hadn't he the right, like other people, to be grumpy on a cold, grey winter's day? He had been like that since morning and it was not particularly unpleasant. One can quite easily be a crosspatch without being unhappy.

He did not like his wife watching him, darting

furtive little glances at him. It gave him a guilty feeling, when he was not guilty of anything. What could he have said to her to reassure her? That Pardon had told him about her visit?

The fact of the matter, as he was only just beginning to realize, was that he was annoyed, even a little sad. All because of his customer that morning. This was the sort of intimate little secret which you tell nobody and which you do not like to confess to yourself.

This fellow, for all that he was a specialist in electric trains, was not a crank, like so many of the people who turn up at the Quai des Orfèvres. He had a problem. He had chosen to explain it frankly to Maigret. Not to any police officer. To Maigret.

And then, when the latter had come back to his office, after going to the chief's room to meet the American, Xavier Marton was no longer there.

He had gone without getting to the end of his confidences. Why? Was he in such a hurry? Wasn't it rather because he had been disappointed?

Before coming, he had formed a definite idea of the chief-inspector. He must have expected understanding, an immediate human contact. He had found a rather dull-witted fellow, stupefied by the warmth from the over-heated radiators, who looked at him without a word of encouragement, and with a wearied or bored expression.

All right, it was nothing. Just a passing shadow. Soon, Maigret would have forgotten all about it.

And at table, he took care to talk about anything but that.

'Don't you think it's time we had a maid? We've got a room on the sixth floor which we've never used for anything . . .'

'And what would she do?'

'The housework, dammit! Or at least the heavy work.'

He would have been wiser not to have broached that particular subject.

'Don't you like your lunch?'

'Yes, I do. The thing is, you're tiring yourself out.'

'I've got a woman who comes two mornings a week to do the cleaning. Will you tell me what I should do with myself all day if I had a maid?'

'You could go out for walks.'

'By myself?'

'There's no reason why you shouldn't have some women friends.'

Good! Now it was his wife's turn to be upset. As she saw things, it was rather as if he wanted to rob her of one of her prerogatives, the one she had most at heart.

'You think I'm growing old?'

'We are all growing old. That isn't what I meant to say. It seemed to me . . .'

There are days like that, when one does everything wrong, with the best will in the world. Once lunch was over, he dialled a number on the telephone. A familiar voice answered. He said:

'Is that you, Pardon?'

And he realized that he had just done another needlessly cruel thing. His wife was looking at him in alarm, telling herself that he had discovered her secret.

'Maigret here.'

'Is there something wrong?'

'No. I'm quite all right . . .'

He hastily added:

'My wife too . . . Look, are you terribly busy?'

Pardon's answer brought a smile to his lips. It was funny, because he could have said exactly the same thing himself.

'Dead calm! In November and December everybody arranged to fall ill at the same time and I didn't have three whole nights in bed. On some days the waiting-room was too small and the telephone never stopped ringing. During the holidays, a few hang-overs and a few liver complaints. And now that people have spent their money, keeping just enough back to pay the rent, they are all well again . . .'

'Could I come round and see you? I'd like to have a chat with you about a case that cropped up this morning at Headquarters.'

'I'll be expecting you.'

'Now?'

'If you like.'

Madame Maigret asked him:

'You're sure it isn't you? You aren't feeling ill?'

'No, I swear I'm not.'

He kissed her, and came back to pat her cheeks and murmur:

28

'Don't you worry. I think I must have got out of bed on the wrong side.'

He made his way leisurely to the Rue Picpus where Pardon lived in an old block of flats without a lift. The maid, who knew him, did not take him through the waiting-room, but along the corridor and in at the back door.

'He won't be a minute. As soon as his patient has gone, I'll show you in.'

He found Pardon in a white coat, in his consulting-room with the frosted-glass windows.

'I hope you haven't told your wife that I let you know about her? She would hold it against me for the rest of her life.'

'I'm delighted that she has decided to take care of herself. You're sure there's nothing seriously wrong?'

'Nothing at all. In a few weeks' time, perhaps three months, when she has lost a few pounds, she'll feel ten years younger.'

Maigret pointed to the waiting-room.

'I'm not taking your patients' time?'

'There are only two of them, and they've got nothing else to do.'

'Do you know a certain Dr. Steiner?'

'The neurologist?'

'Yes. He lives in the Place Denfert-Rochereau.'

'I knew him vaguely at the Medical School, because he's roughly the same age as I am, and after that I lost sight of him. But I've heard about him from my colleagues. He's one of the most brilliant men of his generation. After passing his examinations with every possible distinction, he was first a houseman, then a registrar at Sainte-Anne. Next, he passed his *agrégation* and he might have been expected to become one of the youngest professors.'

'What happened?'

'Nothing. His character. It may be that he's too conscious of his merit. He makes it felt, and likes behaving in a dry, almost arrogant way. At the same time, he's an over-anxious type, for whom every case poses moral problems. During the war, he refused to wear the yellow star, claiming that he hadn't a drop of Jewish blood in him. The Germans finally proved him wrong and sent him off to a concentration camp. He came back from it thoroughly embittered and he imagines that it's on account of his origins that obstructions are put in his way—which is absurd because the Faculty contains a certain number of Jewish professors. You are having some dealings with him?'

'I telephoned him this morning. I wanted some information from him, but I see now that there's no point in pressing for it.'

Rather like his visitor that morning, Maigret did not know where to begin.

'Although this isn't your speciality, I'd like to ask your opinion on a story I've been told lately. I've had in my office a fellow of forty or so, who seems normal and who talked to me without any hysteria, without any exaggeration, weighing his words. He has been married about twelve years, if I remember rightly, and he has been living longer than that in the Avenue de Châtillon.'

Pardon, who had lit a cigarette, was listening attentively.

'His line is electric trains.'

'You mean he's an engineer on the railways?'

'No. I'm talking about toys.'

Pardon frowned.

'I know,' said Maigret. 'That struck me too. But trains aren't just a hobby with him. He's the head salesman in the toy department of a big store and it was he who, among other things, rigged up the electric train in the window display for Christmas. As far as I can judge, he's perfectly fit.'

'What offence has he committed?'

'None. At least, I suppose not. He told me that his wife, for some time past, has been meaning to kill him.'

'How did he find that out?'

'He went off before he could give me any details. All I know is that he found, hidden in a cupboard for brooms and cleaning materials, a bottle containing quite a large quantity of zinc phosphide.'

Pardon became more attentive.

'It was he who had the stuff analysed and he seems to have read up everything there is to read about zinc phosphide. He also brought me a sample of it.'

'You want to know whether it's a poison?'

'I imagine it's a poisonous chemical?'

'Very poisonous and, in certain country districts, they use it to destroy meadow mice. Has he been ill?'

'He has felt unwell several times.'

'Has he laid a complaint?'

'No. He disappeared from my office without telling me what he was getting at. That's precisely what's worrying me.'

'I think I understand. It was he who went to see Steiner? . . . With his wife? . . .'

'No. Alone. He had himself examined, about a month ago, to make sure . . .'

'. . . that he wasn't mad?'

Maigret nodded, lighting his pipe before going on:

'I could summon him to my office, and even have him examined myself, since Steiner is taking refuge behind his professional oath of secrecy. When I say that I could, I'm exaggerating a little because, in point of fact, there's nothing against him. He came to see me of his own free will. He told me a story which sounds reasonable. Neither he nor anyone else has laid a complaint, and there's no law against possessing a certain amount of any poisonous chemical. You see the problem?'

'I see.'

'It may be that his story's true. If I go and see his superiors to ask about his behaviour, I run the risk of doing him harm because, in the big stores, as in the Civil Service, they mistrust people who attract the attention of the police. If I

32

arrange to have his concierge and his neighbours questioned, rumours will spread round his district . . .'

'You realize what you're asking me for, Maigret. An opinion about a man whom I've never seen, whom you don't know, so to speak, yourself. And I'm only a family doctor, with just a vague smattering of neurology and psychiatry.'

'I remember seeing, in your library, a certain number of works on . . .'

'Between being interested in these things and making a diagnosis, there's an enormous gulf. In short, what you'd like to know is why he came and told you his story?'

'That's the first question. He goes on living with his wife and he doesn't appear to be thinking of parting from her. He didn't ask me to arrest her, nor to start an inquiry into her conduct. And, when I had to leave my office for a few minutes, because the chief wanted to see me, he disappeared, as if he didn't want to go any further with his confidences. Does that mean anything to you?'

'It can mean any number of things. You see, Maigret, in the days when I was a student, these questions were much simpler than they are today. Like the whole of medicine, indeed, and like nearly all the sciences. When, in a court of law, they asked an expert whether a man was mad or of sound mind, the expert more often than not replied with a yes or a no. Do you read the criminological journals?'

'Some of them.'

'In that case, you know as well as I do that it isn't so easy nowadays to make a clear distinction between psychoses, neuroses, psychoneuroses and even, sometimes, schizophrenia. The barrier between a man of sound mind and a psychopath or a neuropath is more and more fragile and, if one followed certain foreign specialists . . . But I'm not going to embark on a scientific or pseudo-scientific lecture . . .'

'At first sight . . .'

'At first sight, the answer to your question depends on the specialist to whom you put it. For instance, this business of electric trains, even if that's his occupation—*because he chose that occupation*—can be interpreted as a sign that he's incapable of adapting himself to reality, and that would point to a psycho-neurosis. The fact of his coming to see you at the Quai des Orfèvres and complacently exposing his private life would make any psychiatrist prick up his ears, as would that of his going of his own accord to a neurologist to make sure that he was of sound mind.'

Maigret was not much better off, for he had thought of all this himself.

'You tell me that he was calm, that he spoke deliberately, without obvious emotion, in any case without excessive emotion, and that can just as easily count against him as it can be considered in his favour, like the fact that he had the zinc phosphide analysed and read everything he could about that chemical. He hasn't suggested that his wife was going mad?'

'Not exactly. I can't remember every detail. To tell the truth, at the beginning I was only listening to him with half an ear. It was very warm in my office. I was feeling sleepy . . .'

'If he suspects his wife of being mad, that would be another indication. But it's also quite possible that it's his wife who . . .'

Maigret got up from his armchair and began walking up and down.

'I'd do better not to bother about it,' he grumbled, as much to himself as to his friend Pardon.

He added straight away:

'And yet, I know that I am going to bother about it.'

'It isn't absolutely impossible that the whole thing only exists in his imagination and that he bought the phosphide himself.'

'You can buy it freely?' asked Maigret.

'No. But the shop where he works may have got some to destroy rats, for instance.'

'Let us suppose that that's the case, that Marton belongs to the category you've thought of: is he a dangerous man?'

'He can become one at any moment.'

'And supposing that his wife is really trying to . . .'

Maigret suddenly turned to face the doctor and growled:

'Hell and damnation!'

Then he smiled.

'Forgive me. That wasn't meant for you. We were so peaceful at the Quai. Like you here! The off season, in fact. And then along comes this braggart who sends in a form, sits down in my office and, in the twinkling of an eye, saddles me with responsibilities which . . .'

'You aren't responsible.'

'From the official, professional point of view, no. All the same, if, tomorrow or next week, one of the two, the man or the woman, happens to die, I shall be convinced that it's my fault . . .'

'Sorry, Maigret, that I can't help you any more. Would you like me to try to get in touch with Steiner to ask his opinion?'

Maigret nodded, without conviction. Pardon rang the Place Denfert-Rochereau, then the clinic where Steiner was to be found at that time. Though Pardon spoke humbly and respectfully, as befitted an obscure family doctor addressing a famous specialist, Maigret understood, from his face and from the cutting voice which he heard vibrating in the receiver, that this approach was having no more success than his own.

'He put me in my place.'

'Forgive me.'

'But no! We had to try. Don't worry about it too much. If everybody who behaved in a peculiar way was to become a murderer or a victim, there would be more vacant flats available than there are today.'

Maigret walked as far as the Place de la République, where he caught his bus. At the Quai des Orfèvres, Janvier, who was in the inspectors' office, came over straight away to make his report, wearing a sheepish expression.

'He can't have seen me here, can he?' he said. 'And my photo has never as you might say appeared in the papers. Do I look so very much like a copper?'

Of the whole staff, Janvier was the man who looked least like one.

'I went up to the toy department and I recognized him straight away, from the description you gave me. Over there, he wears a long grey overall, with the firm's initials embroidered in red. An electric train was running, and I watched it working. Then I beckoned to our man and I started asking him a few innocent questions, like a father who's thinking of buying a train for his kid. I know what it's like, because I bought one for my son the Christmas before last. Well, he scarcely let me say three or four sentences. Then he interrupted me and muttered:

' "Tell Chief-Inspector Maigret that it's pretty shabby of him sending you here and that he's running the risk of getting me the sack."

'He spoke almost without moving his lips, and looking anxiously at a shop-walker who was watching us from a distance.'

On the chief-inspector's desk there was a slip of paper from the laboratory with, written on it in red: *zinc phosphide*.

For two pins, Maigret would have let the matter drop. As he had said to Pardon, or as Pardon had said to him, he could not remember exactly which, it did not concern him from the strictly professional point of view and, if he annoyed

Xavier Marton, the latter might very well complain about it and stir up trouble for him.

'I'd like to send you to the Avenue de Châtillon to question the concierge and the neighbours. Only, they mustn't suspect in the district that the police are taking an interest in our man. You might do a bit of door-to-door salesmanship, with a vacuum cleaner, for instance . . .'

Janvier could not help pulling a face at the idea of lugging a vacuum cleaner from house to house.

'If you prefer, you can say you're an insurance agent . . .'

Janvier preferred, obviously.

'Try to find out how they live, what the wife looks like, what people think of them in the district. If the wife is at home, you can always ring and offer her a life-assurance policy. . . .'

'I'll do my best, Chief.'

The weather was still just as grey, just as cold, and the office, in which the chief-inspector had forgotten to switch the radiator on again, was almost freezing. He went and turned the handle, wondering for a moment whether to go and ask the chief's advice. If he did not do so, it was for fear of looking ridiculous. He had realized, while he was telling the story to Pardon, how little he had to go on.

Slowly filling a pipe, he immersed himself once more in the file which he had abandoned that morning and in which he could not succeed in summoning up any interest. An hour went by.

The air became more opaque, because of the smoke and the falling dusk. He lit the lamp with the green shade, and got up to regulate the radiator, which was once more getting out of control. There was a knock at the door. Old Joseph put a form on the corner of the desk, murmuring:

'A lady.'

She must have impressed the old porter, for him to use that particular word.

Joseph added:

'I think it's the wife of the chap who came this morning.'

The name written on the form had reminded him of something: 'Madame Marton.' And, underneath, the word 'personal' had been entered below the words 'Purpose of Call'.

'Where is she?'

'In the waiting-room. Shall I show her in?'

He nearly said yes, then thought better of it.

'No. I'll see to her myself.'

He took his time, going through the inspectors' office, then two other offices, so as not to come out into the vast corridor until he was on the other side of the glazed waiting-room. As it was not yet completely dark, the lamps seemed to be shedding less light than usual, and the atmosphere was as yellowish and dismal as in a little provincial railway station.

From a doorway, he inspected the aquarium-like room, in which there were only three people, two of whom were obviously there to see the Vice Squad, for one of them was a little pimp who had Place Pigalle written all over him, and the other was a buxom young woman who had all the self-assurance of a regular customer.

Both of them kept glancing at another woman who was waiting there and who looked out of place on account of her simple yet faultless elegance.

Maigret, taking his time, finally got to the glass door and opened it.

'Madame Marton?'

He had noticed the crocodile handbag matching the shoes, the severe costume under a beaver fur coat.

She got up with just the right degree of confusion one would expect in somebody who had never had anything to do with the police and suddenly found herself faced with one of their most important representatives.

'It's Chief-Inspector Maigret, isn't it?'

The other two, old customers that they were, exchanged meaning looks. Maigret showed her into his office, and gave her the armchair which her husband had occupied that morning.

'I must apologize for bothering you like this . . .'

She took off her right glove, which was made of soft suède, and crossed her legs.

'I suppose you can guess why I'm here?'

It was she who was attacking and Maigret did not like that. Accordingly he refrained from answering.

'Doubtless you too are going to talk to me about professional secrecy . . .'

He noticed particularly the *you too*. Did that mean that she had been to see Dr. Steiner?

It was not only by her attitude that Madame Marton surprised him.

The husband, it was true, was not at all bad-looking, and he presumably made a decent living. Madame Marton belonged none the less to a different class. Her elegance had nothing forced, nothing vulgar about it. Nor had her self-assurance.

Already, in the waiting-room, he had noticed the perfect cut of her shoes and the richness of her hand-bag. Her gloves were not of inferior quality, nor was the rest of what she was wearing. Nothing aggressive, nothing obvious. No showiness. Everything she was wearing had come from excellent shops.

She too looked about forty, that special forty peculiar to Parisian women who take care of their appearance and, in her voice as in her behaviour, she gave the impression of someone who is at ease everywhere and under all circumstances.

Was there really a flaw? He thought he could sense one, a very small discordant note, but he was incapable of putting his finger on it. It was an impression rather than something he had observed.

'I think, Chief-Inspector, that it would save time if I spoke frankly to you. In any case it would be presumptuous to try any artful tricks with a man like you.'

He remained impassive, but this impassivity

did not worry her, or else she had marvellous self-control.

'I know that my husband came to see you this morning.'

He finally opened his mouth, hoping to startle her.

'Did he tell you so?' he asked.

'No. I saw him entering this building and I realized that it was you he had come to see. He takes a passionate interest in all your cases. For years he has spoken enthusiastically about you on every possible occasion.'

'You mean to say that you followed your husband?'

'Yes,' she admitted simply.

There was a short and rather embarrassed silence.

'Does that surprise you, after seeing and hearing him?'

'Do you also know what he said to me?'

'I can easily guess. We've been married now for twelve years and I know Xavier well. He's the most honest, the most courageous, the most likeable person imaginable. You probably know that he never knew his parents and that he was brought up by the Board of Guardians?'

He gave a slight nod of the head.

'He was brought up on a farm in Sologne, where they snatched out of his hands and burnt any books that he managed to get hold of. He has none the less arrived where he is now and, in my opinion, he's a long way from having the job he deserves. For my part, I'm constantly surprised by the extent of his knowledge. He has read everything. He knows about everything. And, of course, people take advantage of him. He kills himself over his work. Six months before Christmas he's already getting ready for the festive season, and the season, for him, is exhausting.'

She had opened her handbag, and was hesitating whether to take out a silver cigarette-case.

'You may smoke,' he said.

'Thank you. It's a bad habit of mine. I smoke far too much. I hope my presence isn't preventing you from lighting your pipe?'

He could make out some fine crow's-feet at the corners of her eyelids, but, instead of making her look older, this lent her an added charm. Her grey-blue eyes had the gentle sparkle that comes from short sight.

'We must seem ridiculous to you, the two of us, I mean my husband and I, coming here in turn as if we were coming to confession. It's rather like that when you come to think of it. For months, I've been concerned about my husband. He's over-worked and worried, with periods of utter despondency during which he doesn't say a word to me.'

Maigret would have liked Pardon to be present, for perhaps the doctor would have been able to make something out of this.

'Already in October . . . yes, at the beginning of October . . . I told him that he was getting neurotic and that he ought to go and see a doctor . . .'

'It was you who mentioned neurosis to him?'

'Yes. Shouldn't I have done so?'

'Go on.'

'I watched him a great deal. He began by complaining about one of his superiors whom he has never liked. But, for the first time, he spoke of a sort of conspiracy. Then he started going for a young salesman . . .'

'What about?'

'This sounds ridiculous, but to a certain extent I understand Xavier's reactions. I'm not exaggerating when I say that he is, in France, the greatest specialist in electric trains. I hope that doesn't make you smile? People don't make fun of someone who, for instance, spends his life designing brassières or corsets.'

Why did he ask:

'Do you have something to do with brassières and corsets?'

She laughed.

'I sell them. But I wasn't talking about myself. As I was saying, the new salesman started watching my husband, worming his little tricks out of him, designing circuits. . . . In short, he gave him the impression that he was out to take his place. . . . I only really began worrying when I saw that Xavier's suspicions were extending to me . . .'

'What did he suspect you of?'

'I imagine he has told you. It all began one evening when, looking at me closely, he murmured:

' "You'd make a beautiful widow, wouldn't you?"

'That word often came up again in conversations. For example:

' "All women are made to be widows. Besides, statistics prove . . ."

'You see the theme. From there to telling me that without him, I should have a more brilliant career, that he was the only obstacle to my success . . .'

She did not falter, despite the expressionless gaze which Maigret deliberately brought to bear on her.

'You know the rest. He's convinced that I've decided to get rid of him. At table, he's apt to exchange his glass for mine without concealing what he's doing, gazing at me on the contrary with a mocking expression. Before eating, he waits until I've swallowed the first mouthful. Sometimes, when I come home after him, I find him hunting about all over the kitchen.

'I don't know what Dr. Steiner said to him . . .'

'Did you go there with him?'

'No. Xavier told me that he was going to go and see him. Again, it was a sort of challenge on his part. He said to me:

' "I know that you're trying to convince me that I'm going mad. Oh, you're going about it very cleverly, drop by drop, so to speak. But we shall see what a specialist has to say about it." '

'Did he tell you the result of the consultation?'

'He told me nothing, but, since then—it was about a month ago—he has been looking at me with an air of ironical superiority. I don't know if you can understand what I mean. Like a man who has a secret and who's gloating over it. He follows me with his eyes. All the time I have the impression that he's thinking:

' "Go on, my girl! Do what you like. You won't succeed, because I know what you're up to . . ." '

Maigret sucked his pipe and said:

'So this morning you followed him. Are you in the habit of following him?'

'Not every day, no, because I have my own work too. Usually, we set off together, at half past eight, from the Avenue de Châtillon, and we take the same bus as far as the Rue des Pyramides. Then I go to the shop, in the Rue Saint-Honoré, while he carries on along the Rue de Rivoli as far as the Magasins du Louvre. Well, for some time, as I've already mentioned, I think, your name has been cropping up fairly frequently in conversation. Two days ago, he said to me, in a voice that was sardonic and threatening at the same time:

' "Whatever you do, however cunning you are, there will be somebody who will know all about it." '

She added:

'I realized that it was you he meant. Yesterday, already, I followed him as far as the Louvre and stayed for some time watching the staff entrance, to make sure that he didn't come out again. This morning, I did the same . . .'

'And you followed him here?'

She said yes, openly, and bent forward to stub out her cigarette in the glass ash-tray.

'I've tried to give you some idea of the situation. Now, I am ready to answer your questions.'

Only her hands, folded on top of the crocodile handbag betrayed a certain nervousness.

3

IF, that morning, he had been dull-witted and absent-minded when faced with the electric-train salesman, it had been an involuntary dullness, something more akin to torpor, to a sort of somnolence. Contact, in fact, had not been established; or to be more precise, it had been established too late.

At present, with Madame Marton, it was his professional dullness that he had recovered, the dullness which he had assumed long ago, when he was still shy, in order to mislead the people he had to talk to, and which had become an almost unconscious reflex.

She did not seem to be impressed by it and went on looking at him in the way a child looks at a big bear which does not frighten him, but which he watches none the less out of the corner of his eye.

Wasn't it she who, so far, had conducted the conversation, ending up with a remark which Maigret had rarely heard in this office of his:

'Now, I await your questions . . .'

He made her wait for some time, deliberately letting the silence deepen, pulling at his pipe, and finally saying with the air of someone who does not quite know what he is doing:

'Exactly why have you come to tell me all this?'

And that did indeed throw her off her balance. She began:

'But . . .'

She fluttered her eyelashes like a short-sighted person, failed to think of anything else to say, and gave a little smile to suggest that the answer was obvious.

He went on, as if he attached no importance to the matter, as if he were a civil servant doing a routine duty:

'Are you asking us to have your husband certified?'

This time, her face immediately flushed scarlet, her eyes glazed and her lips quivered with anger.

'I don't remember saying anything which would entitle you to . . .'

The thrust had gone so deep that she made as if to get up and bring the conversation to an end.

'Sit down, please. Compose yourself. I don't see why such a perfectly natural question should upset you like that. In point of fact, what did you come here to tell me? Don't forget that here we are at Police Headquarters, where our business is with crimes and misdemeanours, either trying to arrest the culprits, or, more rarely, trying to prevent the crimes themselves. First of all, you told me that, for several months, your husband has seemed to be getting neurotic . . .'

'I said . . .'

'You said neurotic. And his behaviour worried you so much that you sent him to see a neurologist . . .'

'I advised him . . .'

'Let us say you advised him to consult a neurologist. Did you expect the neurologist to say that he ought to be certified?'

Her features drawn, her voice changed, she retorted:

'I expected him to look after my husband.'

'Good. I suppose he did?'

'I have no idea.'

'You rang up Dr. Steiner, or you went to see him, and he took refuge behind his oath of professional secrecy.'

She was looking at him with unremitting attention, her nerves keyed up, as if to guess what the next attack was going to be.

'Since his visit to the doctor, has your husband been taking any medicine?'

'Not as far as I know.'

'Has his behaviour altered?'

'He still seems to me to be just as depressed as before.'

'Depressed, but not excited?'

'I don't know. I don't see what you're driving at.'

'What are you afraid of?'

This time, it was she who took her time, asking herself what the question referred to.

'Are you asking me whether I'm afraid of my husband?'

'Yes.'

'I'm afraid *for* him. I'm not afraid *of* him.'

'Why not?'

'Because, whatever happens, I'm capable of defending myself.'

'In that case, I come back to what I asked you at the beginning. Why did you come to see me this afternoon?'

'Because he came to see you this morning.'

They did not reason the same way, the two of them. Or was it that she did not want to reason the same way as the chief-inspector?

'Did you know what he was going to tell me?'

'If I'd known that, I . . .'

She bit her lip. Wasn't she going on to say:

'. . . I wouldn't have had to bother.'

Maigret did not have time to think about it, for the telephone on his desk started ringing. He picked up the receiver.

'Hullo, Chief . . . Janvier here . . . I'm in the office next door . . . They told me who you were with and I thought it best not to show my face . . . I'd like to talk to you for a moment . . .'

'I'm coming.'

He got up and apologized.

'Will you excuse me? Someone needs to see me about another business. I shan't be long.'

In the inspectors' office he said to Lucas:

'Go into the corridor and, if she tries to get away like her husband, stop her.'

He had shut the communicating door. Torrence had had a glass of beer sent up and, automatically, Maigret drank it with relish.

'You've got some news?'

'I've been over there. You know the Avenue de Châtillon. You might think yourself in the provinces, for all that the Avenue d'Orléans is so close. No. 17, where they live, is a new block of flats, with seven stories, in yellow brick, and the tenants are mostly office workers and commercial travellers.

'You must be able to hear everything that's going on in the next flat, and there are kids on every floor.

'The Martons don't live in the apartment-house proper. Where it stands there used to be a sort of big private house which has been demolished. The courtyard is still there, with a tree in the middle and, at the far end, a two-floored cottage.

'An outside staircase goes up to the first floor, where there are only two bedrooms and a bathroom.

'Eighteen years ago, when Xavier Marton, who was still a bachelor, rented this place, the ground floor, which has a glass front, was a carpenter's workshop.

'Later, the carpenter disappeared, Marton rented the ground floor and turned it into an attractive room, half studio, half living-room.

'The over-all effect is unusual, stylish, amusing. It isn't an ordinary house. I started by offering a life-assurance policy to the concierge, who listened to my patter without interrupting me, only to tell me at the end that she didn't need one because she would have her old-age pension one day. I asked if there were any tenants who might be interested. She mentioned a few names.

' "They're all in social insurance schemes," she added. "You haven't got much hope . . ."

' "Haven't you got a Monsieur Marton?"

' "At the far end of the courtyard, yes . . . Perhaps they might . . . They make a decent living . . . Last year, they bought a car . . . Yes, try them . . ."

' "Will there be anybody at home?"

' "I think so."

'As you can see, Chief, it wasn't too difficult. I rang at the studio door. A youngish woman answered the bell.

' "Madame Marton?" I asked.

' "No. My sister won't be back till about seven." '

Maigret had started frowning.

'What's the sister like?'

'A woman men are bound to turn round and look at in the street. Speaking for myself . . .'

'You were impressed?'

'She's difficult to describe. I should say she was about thirty-five at the outside. It isn't that she's pretty, or striking. I wasn't impressed by her elegance, either, because she was wearing a little black woollen dress and her hair was untidy—like any woman doing the housework. Only . . .'

'Only?'

'Well, there's something very feminine about her, something touching. You feel that she's very sweet, a little frightened by life, and that's the kind of woman a man wants to protect. You know what I mean? Her figure too is very feminine, very . . .'

He blushed at Maigret's smile of amusement.

'Did you stay with her for long?'

'Ten minutes or so. I talked about insurance to begin with. She replied that her brother-in-law and her sister had both taken out heavy insurance policies about a year ago . . .'

'She didn't specify the amount?'

'No. All I know is that it was with the Mutual. She added that, for her part, she doesn't need any insurance, because she has a pension. Alongside one of the walls there's a table, with a complicated electric train on it, close to a workbench. I said that I'd just bought my son an electric train. That enabled me to stay there longer. She asked if I'd bought the train at the Magasins du Louvre and I said yes.

' "In that case, it must have been my brother-in-law who served you . . ." '

'That's all?' asked Maigret.

'Just about. I saw two or three shopkeepers, but I didn't dare to be too precise. The Martons seem to be well thought of in the district and to pay their bills promptly.'

Only now did Maigret notice that it was Torrence's glass he had emptied.

'I beg your pardon, old man. Have another one sent up at my expense. . . .'

He added:

'And one for me. I'll come and drink it when I've finished with this customer of mine.'

The latter, during his absence, had not stirred from her armchair, but had lit a cigarette.

He sat down again, his hands flat on the desk.

'I can't remember where we were. Oh, yes! You'd invited me to question you. But I don't really see what I can ask you. Have you got a maid, Madame Marton? Because, if I've understood you rightly, you work all day?'

'All day, yes.'

'On your own account?'

'Not exactly. All the same, my employer, Monsieur Harris, who started the lingerie shop in the Rue Saint-Honoré, gives me quite a high percentage of the profits, because I'm the one who really runs the business.'

'So you have a very good position?'

'Quite good, yes.'

'I seem to have heard of the Maison Harris.'

'It's one of the three best in Paris for fine lingerie. We have a high-class clientèle, including several crowned heads.'

He began to understand certain details which had struck him at the beginning, the discreet yet rather unusual elegance of his visitor. As often happens in fashion houses and certain branches of business, she had gradually acquired the tastes and the attitudes of her clientèle, while at the same time retaining a certain indispensable modesty.

'Your parents were in the lingerie business?'

She relaxed, now that they were on more ordinary ground and the questions appeared to be innocent.

'Far from it. My father was a history master at the Rouen *lycée*, and my mother did nothing all her life apart from being a general's daughter.'

'Have you any brothers and sisters?'

'A sister, who lived for some time in the United States, at Green Village, in New Jersey, not far from New York, with her husband. Her husband was an engineer in a petrol-refining company.'

'You say: was?'

'He was killed two years ago in an explosion in the laboratories. My sister came back to France, so unsettled, so depressed, that we took her in.'

'I asked you just now whether you had a maid.'

'No. My sister doesn't go out to work. She has never done any work in her life. She's younger than I am and married at twenty, while she was still living with my parents. She has always been a spoilt child.'

'It's your sister who keeps house for you?'

'It's her way, if you like, of paying her share. It wasn't we who asked her to do it, but she who insisted.'

'You were living with your parents too when you met your husband?'

'No. Unlike Jenny—that's my sister—I didn't feel that I was made to live in Rouen and I didn't get on very well with my mother. As soon as I'd got my baccalaureate I came to Paris.'

'By yourself?'

'What do you mean?'

'You hadn't got a friend here?'

'I see what you're driving at. Since I asked you to question me, I haven't any excuse for not answering you. I came here, it is true, to join someone I knew, a young lawyer, and we lived together for a few months. That didn't work and I started looking for a job. I then discovered that the baccalaureate, which my father was so keen on that he martyred me for years on end, was no use whatever. All that I could find, after weeks of coming and going in Paris, was a post as a saleswoman at the Magasins du Louvre.'

'And then you met Marton.'

'Not straight away. We weren't in the same department. It was in the Metro that we finally made each other's acquaintance.'

'He was already a head salesman?'

'No, of course not.'

'You got married?'

'He was the one who wanted to. As for myself, I should have been content to have lived with him . . .'

'You love him?'

'Why should I be here if I didn't?'

'When did you leave the shop?'

'Wait a minute. . . . It will be five years ago next month.'

'That's to say, after seven years of marriage.'

'About that.'

'And, by that time, your husband had become the head of a department?'

'Yes.'

'But you were still just an ordinary sales-woman.'

'I don't see what you're driving at.'

He murmured, absent-mindedly:

'Nor do I. So then you entered Monsieur Harris's service.'

'It didn't happen quite like that. In the first place, Harris is the name of the firm. My employer's real name is Maurice Schwob. He used to work at the Magasins du Louvre, where he was the buyer in lingerie.'

'What age?'

'Now?'

'Yes.'

'Forty-nine. But it isn't what you think. Our relations are on a purely business footing. He'd always intended to set up on his own account. He needed a young woman in the shop who knew the business. When it comes to lingerie and corsets, women don't like being served by a man. He'd noticed me at the Louvre. That's all there is to it.'

'You are practically partners?'

'In a sense, yes, although my stake in the business is much smaller than his, which is natural enough, seeing that he supplied the capital and it's he who designs the models.'

'In short, until about five years ago, your husband's position was much better than yours. His pay too. But for the past five years, the reverse has been the case. Is that correct?'

'That is correct, yes, but please believe me when I say that I don't so much as give it a thought.'

'Your husband doesn't give it a thought, either?'

She hesitated.

'To begin with, a man doesn't like it. He has got used to it. We continue to live a quiet life.'

'You have a car?'

'That's true, but we scarcely ever use it except at week-ends and in the holidays.'

'You go on holiday with your sister?'

'Why not?'

'Why not, indeed?'

There was quite a long silence. Maigret looked embarrassed.

'Now that I can't think of any other questions to ask you, tell me, Madame Marton, what you want me to do.'

This was enough to put her on the defensive once more.

'I still don't understand,' she murmured.

'You don't want us to watch your husband?'

'Why watch him?'

'You aren't prepared to sign a formal application which would enable us to have him examined by a mental specialist?'

'Certainly not.'

'Then that's all?'

'That's all . . . I suppose.'

'In that case, I don't see, either, why I should detain you any longer. . . .'

He got up. She copied him, a little stiffly. Just as he was about to show her to the door, he appeared to change his mind.

'Do you use zinc phosphide?'

She did not start. She must have been expecting that question all the time, and who knows if she hadn't come in order to answer it?

'I use some, yes.'

'What for?'

'The Rue Saint-Honoré is one of the oldest streets in Paris and behind the luxury shops, the houses are mostly in poor condition; there's a whole network of courtyards, alleys and passages which you'd never dream existed. The nearness of the market too attracts an incredible number of rats and these have caused damage to our stock. We've tried several products without success. Someone advised Monsieur Schwob to use zinc phosphide, which has produced excellent results.

'In the Avenue de Châtillon too we had some rats, and my husband used to complain about them. I took a certain amount of phosphide from the shop . . .'

'Without telling your husband?'

'I can't remember now whether I told him or not.'

She opened her eyes wide, as if an idea had struck her.

'I suppose he can't have imagined . . . ?'

He did not finish the sentence for her and she went on:

'If he spoke to you about it, it means that . . . Heavens above! And there was I racking my brains to guess what was worrying him . . . I must have it out with him tonight . . . Or rather . . . If I bring that subject up, he'll know that I've been to see you. . . .'

'You expected to be able to keep it from him?'

'I don't know, I don't know any more, Monsieur Maigret. I came here . . . how shall I put it? . . . I came here in all simplicity, with the idea—a naïve idea, I know—of confiding in you. I told you the truth about Xavier and about my worries. Instead of helping me, you have asked me questions which, I can see, show that you don't believe me, that you suspect me of heaven knows what intentions . . .'

She was not crying, but she was none the less showing signs of a certain distress.

'Well, it can't be helped! . . . I had hoped . . . All that I can do now is try my best . . .'

She opened the door with her gloved hand. Standing in the corridor, she said again:

'Good-bye, Chief-Inspector. . . . Thank you all the same for being good enough to see me . . .'

Maigret watched her walking away with neat steps, perched on very high heels, and he shrugged his shoulders as he went back into his office. A good quarter of an hour had passed before he came out again and made for the chief's office, asking Joseph on the way:

'Is the Director in?'

'No. He's in conference with the Prefect and told me that he probably wouldn't come back this afternoon.'

All the same Maigret went into the office of the Director of Police Headquarters, turned on the light, and began reading the titles of the works which filled the two mahogany book-cases. There were statistical works which nobody had ever opened, and technical books in several languages which the authors or publishers had sent as a matter of course. There were numerous treatises on criminology, as also on scientific detection and forensic medicine.

Maigret finally found on one shelf several works on psychiatry and skimmed through three or four before picking one which seemed to him to be written in simpler and more comprehensible language than the others.

That evening, he took the book home with him. After dinner, sitting in his slippers in front of the log fire, with the radio playing quietly in the background, he started reading, while Madame Maigret mended shirt cuffs.

He had no intention of reading the bulky volume from cover to cover and there were whole pages which, in spite of his brief medical studies, he was incapable of understanding.

He looked for certain chapter headings, certain words which had been used that morning in the course of his conversation with Pardon, words whose meaning everybody thinks he knows but which, for professionals, have a very different resonance.

. . . Neuroses . . . In Adler's opinion, the starting-point of neurosis is an alarming feeling of inferiority and insecurity . . . A defensive reaction against this feeling leads the patient to identify himself with an imaginary ideal. . . .

He repeated under his breath, thus causing his wife to raise her head:

'. . . imaginary ideal . . .'

. . . Physical syndrome . . . Neurasthenics are well known to specialists of every sort . . . Without any appreciable organic lesion, they feel ill and above all worry about possible complications; they undergo innumerable consultations and examinations. . . .

. . . Mental syndrome . . . The feeling of incapacity is dominant . . . Physically, the patient feels dull-witted, full of aches and pains, exhausted by the slightest effort. . . .

Like Maigret that very morning. Even now, he felt dull-witted, not full of aches and pains perhaps, but . . .

He turned the pages, in a grumpy mood.

. . . So-called paranoiac constitution . . . Hypertrophy of the Ego. . . .

. . . Unlike the sensitive type, these patients project

into family and above all social life a personality, an Ego, which is clumsy and domineering. . . .

. . . Never do they consider themselves blamewor- thy or at fault . . . Their pride is characteristic . . . Even when they are not very intelligent, they often dominate their family by means of the authoritari- anism and their arrogant dogmatism. . . .

Did that apply best to Xavier Marton, or to his wife? And couldn't it serve to describe a quarter of the population of Paris?

Revenge psychosis . . . persecuted persecutors . . .

. . . This is a typical emotional psychosis of which the nosological setting has aroused interminable dis- cussions . . . Like Kraepelin and Capgras, I consider that it does not belong to the class of true delu- sions . . . The patient considers himself to be the vic- tim of an injustice which he wishes to redress, and attempts to obtain satisfaction at any price. . . .

Xavier Marton? Madame Marton?

He went from neuroses to psychoses, from psychoses to psychoneuroses, from hysteria to paranoia, and, like those good folk who when they immerse themselves in a medical dictionary discover that they are suffering from each illness in turn, he found, under every heading symp- toms which would apply just as well to the one as to the other of his two characters.

From time to time he grunted, or repeated a word or a phrase, and Madame Maigret darted anxious little glances at him.

In the end he got up, like someone who has had enough, threw the book on to the table and, opening the sideboard in the dining-room, took the bottle of *prunelle* and filled one of the little gilt-edged glasses.

It was a sort of protest on behalf of common sense against all this learned rubbish, a way of getting back to earth with both feet firmly on the ground.

Pardon was right: the result of too much studying of the anomalies of human behaviour, classifying them and subdividing them, was that you ended up not knowing what a man of sound mind was like any more.

Was he one himself? After what he had just been reading, he was not so sure.

'Have you got a difficult case on?' ventured Madame Maigret, who rarely bothered about her husband's work at the Quai des Orfèvres.

He contented himself with shrugging his shoulders and growling:

'A mad business!'

A little later, after emptying his glass, he added:

'Let's go to bed.'

The next morning, however, he asked to see the Director a few minutes before the daily report, and the chief saw straight away that he was worried.

'What's the matter, Maigret?'

He tried to tell him the story of the two calls as succinctly as possible. The chief's first reaction was to look at him in some surprise.

'I don't see what's bothering you. Seeing that no formal complaint has been made to us . . .'

'Quite. Each came to tell me his or her little

story. And neither story, in itself, is really alarming. But, as soon as you try to superimpose them, you realize that they don't fit . . . Incidentally, I'm returning your book.'

He put it on the desk and the Director glanced at the title, then looked at the chief-inspector in even greater surprise.

'Let me make myself clear, Chief. And don't imagine that I've allowed this book to carry me away. I don't say that one of the two is absolutely mad. All the same, there's something wrong somewhere. It's not for nothing that two people, husband and wife, come to see me the same day as if they were coming to confession. And if, tomorrow or in a week, or in a month from now, we found we had a corpse on our hands, I wouldn't feel I had a clear conscience . . .'

'You think that will happen?'

'I don't know. I do and I don't. It's like working on a case the wrong way round. Usually, we have a crime to begin with, and it's only after it's been committed that we have to hunt for the motives. This time, we've got the motives, but so far no crime.'

'Don't you think there are thousands of cases where the motives aren't followed by a crime?'

'I'm sure there are. Only, in those cases, people don't come and tell me their motives *beforehand*.'

The chief thought for a moment.

'I'm beginning to understand.'

'As things are at the moment, there's nothing I can do. Especially after the recent campaign in the Press about the liberties the police have been taking with suspects.'

'Well then?'

'I came to ask you for permission to mention it on the off-chance to the Public Prosecutor.'

'To get him to order an investigation?'

'Something like that. In any case, to set my conscience at rest.'

'I doubt if it will come off.'

'So do I.'

'Go ahead if it will make you happier.'

'Thank you, Chief.'

He had not said exactly what he had promised himself he would say. This was doubtless because it was too complicated, still obscure. Whereas the day before, at this time, he had never heard of the Martons, the specialist in electric trains was beginning to haunt his thoughts, and also the elegant young wife who, he admitted to himself, had stood up to him bravely although he had done everything he could to shake her.

Even the widowed sister-in-law, a touching figure according to Janvier, was engrossing him as if he had always known her.

'Hullo! Maigret here. Will you ask the Public Prosecutor for me if he can spare me a minute or two? . . . This morning, if possible, yes . . . Hullo! I'll hold the line.'

The Public Prosecutor's office was in the *Palais*

de Justice too, in the same buildings, but in a different world, where the walls were covered with carved panelling and where people talked in velvet voices.

'Straight away? . . . Yes . . . I'm coming. . . .'

He went through the glass door separating the two worlds, passed some barristers in black robes, and noticed, waiting between a couple of gendarmes beside nameless doors, people who had gone through his hands a few weeks or a few months before. Some of them looked pleased to see him again and said good morning to him in an almost familiar way.

'If you will wait a moment, the Public Prosecutor will see you straight away. . . .'

It was almost as awe-inspiring as going into the headmaster's study at school.

'Come in, Maigret . . . You wanted to see me? . . . But there's nothing new, is there?'

'I wanted to consult you on a matter which is almost a matter of conscience . . .'

He told the story very badly, much worse even than to the Director of Police Headquarters.

'If I understand you correctly, you're under the impression that there may be an incident, or perhaps a crime?'

'That's roughly it.'

'But this impression is based on nothing specific, apart from a man's vague confidences and the explanation his wife came and gave you afterwards of her own accord? Tell me, Maigret, how many lunatics, semi-lunatics, maniacs and common-or-garden cranks do you see every year in your office?'

'Hundreds . . .'

'And here, I get thousands of letters from the very same people.'

The Public Prosecutor looked at him in silence, as if he had said everything there was to say.

'All the same, I'd like to have carried out an investigation,' the chief-inspector murmured timidly.

'What sort of investigation? Let's be precise. Questioning the neighbours, the employers, the sister-in-law, the tradesmen, and heaven knows who else? In the first place, I don't see what good that will do you. And secondly, if the Martons are trouble-makers, they'll have a perfect right to complain . . .'

'I know . . .'

'As for forcing them, either of them, to be examined by a psychiatrist, we can't do that as long as we haven't received a formal request to that effect from the husband or the wife. And even then . . . !'

'And if a crime is committed . . .'

A short silence. A slight shrug of the shoulders.

'That would be regrettable, of course, but there's nothing we could do about it. And at least, in that event, we shouldn't have far to go to find the culprit.'

'Will you allow me all the same to have them kept under observation?'

'On condition, first of all, that it is done discreetly enough not to get us into trouble. And on a second condition, and that is that it doesn't force you to use inspectors who would be more usefully employed somewhere else . . .'

'We are in a period of dead calm . . .'

'That sort of period never lasts long. If you really want to know my opinion, you're letting your scruples run away with you. In your place, Maigret, I would let the matter drop. Once again, as things are at the moment, we have no right to intervene, and no means of doing so either. These cases of a husband and wife suspecting each other—I'm convinced there are thousands of them all around us . . .'

'But neither the husband nor the wife has ever appealed to me before.'

'Have these two really appealed to you?'

He had to admit that they had not. Marton had not asked him for anything, when it came to the point. Nor had Madame Marton. Sister Jenny even less.

'Forgive me if I don't keep you any longer. There are five or six people waiting to see me and I have an appointment at the Ministry at eleven.'

'I am sorry to have disturbed you.'

Maigret was not pleased with himself. He had the impression that he had stated his case badly. Perhaps he ought not to have immersed himself, the night before, in that treatise on psychiatry.

He walked towards the door. The Public Prosecutor called him back at the last moment, and his tone was no longer the same, his voice was suddenly as cold as when he pronounced one of his famous indictments.

'It is clearly understood that I don't give you any cover at all and that I've forbidden you, until some fresh development occurs, to do anything about this affair?'

'Very good, sir.'

And, in the corridor, head down, he growled:

'. . . fresh development . . . fresh development . . .'

Who was to be the *fresh development*, in other words the victim? He or she?

He shut the glass door so hard that he nearly broke the panes.

4

I T was not the first time, nor in all probability would it be the last, that Maigret had flown into a temper on leaving the Public Prosecutor's office, and his differences with certain judges, particularly Judge Coméliau, who for over twenty years had been as it were his private enemy, were a legend at the Quai des Orfèvres.

In his more collected moments, he did not take too seriously the antagonism which existed between the two worlds. On their different sides of the glass door, each did its job more or less conscientiously. The same people—delinquents, criminals, suspects and witnesses—passed in turn through their hands.

What distinguished them most of all from each other, what created hidden conflicts between them, was the point of view each adopted—a point of view which was probably determined by their different methods of recruitment. The people in the Parquet—attorneys, deputies and examining magistrates—nearly all belonged to the middle, if not the upper, strata of the *bourgeoisie*. Their way of life, after a period of purely theoretical study, scarcely ever brought them into contact, except in their chambers, with those whom they had to prosecute in the name of society.

Hence their well-nigh congenital incomprehension of certain problems, their irritating attitude towards certain cases which the men of Police Headquarters, living in permanent and almost physical intimacy with the criminal world, appraised instinctively.

There was also a certain tendency, in the *Palais de Justice*, to hypocrisy. In spite of their apparent independence, which they talked about a great deal, they were more afraid than anyone else of the Minister's frown and, if a case which aroused public interest was hanging fire, they would spur on the police, who never went fast enough for their liking. It was for the police to make their plans and use what methods they thought fit.

But if the newspapers came to criticize those methods, then the magistrates of the Parquet were quick to share their indignation.

It was not for nothing that the chief-inspector had gone to see the Public Prosecutor. As happens periodically, they were in a tight corner. There had been an incident, for which not Police

Headquarters, fortunately, but the Sûreté Générale, of the Rue des Saussaies, was to blame, and which had assumed serious proportions, giving rise to questions in the Chamber.

In a night-club, the son of a Deputy had made a violent attack on an inspector who, he alleged, had been following him for several days. A general free-for-all had followed. It had proved impossible to hush up the affair and the Sûreté had been forced to admit that it had been making inquiries about the young man who was suspected not only of being a heroin addict, but also of acting as a tout for drug traffickers.

The result had been a sickening show-down. According to the Deputy whose son had been convicted, one of the traffickers was a police spy, and the father alleged that it was with premeditation, on instructions from the Place Beauvau, in order to compromise him, the Deputy, in his political career, that the young man had been turned into a drug addict.

As if by chance—these things never come singly—there had been a case, the following week, of someone being beaten up in a police station.

For some time, therefore, the police had been having a bad Press, and, Maigret, that morning, had preferred to take precautions.

Back in his office, he was none the less determined to get round the instructions he had been given, especially as instructions of that sort are never intended to be taken literally. The Public Prosecutor had been covering himself, that was all, and if, the next day, a corpse was found in the Avenue de Châtillon, he would be the first to blame the chief-inspector for his inactivity.

Since he had to cheat, he cheated, but half-heartedly. He would no longer use Janvier whom, curiously enough, Marton had spotted straight away in the Magasins du Louvre, and who had already shown his face in the Martons' house.

Of all the others, it was Lucas who would have shown the greatest flair and judgment, but Lucas had one great fault: it was easy to guess his profession.

He picked young Lapointe, who had less training and less experience, but who often passed for a student or a young clerk.

'Listen, my lad . . .'

He gave him his instructions at length and at leisure, with all the more details in that these instructions, at bottom, were vague. First of all he was to buy a toy of some sort, without hanging about, without making a fuss, at the Magasins du Louvre, in order to register Marton's appearance so that he would know him again.

Then, at lunch-time, he was to stand close to the staff entrance and shadow the specialist in electric trains.

At night, he was to do it again, if need be. Meanwhile, in the afternoon, he was to go and have a look at the lingerie shop in the Rue Saint-Honoré.

'For all they know, you might be engaged . . .'

Lapointe blushed, for this was almost the case. Almost, but not quite, for the engagement was not yet official.

'You could buy, say, a nightdress for your fiancée. Preferably not too dear . . .'

To which Lapointe shyly retorted:

'You think it's done to give a nightdress to one's fiancée? Isn't it rather intimate?'

Afterwards they would see how they could find out more about the Martons and the young sister-in-law, without giving themselves away.

When Lapointe had gone, Maigret set to work signing documents and letters, listening to his inspectors' reports on minor matters. Marton and his wife remained none the less, like a backcloth, behind his preoccupations of the moment.

He had one faint hope, on which he was not counting too heavily and that was that he would be told that Xavier Marton was asking to see him.

Why not? If he had gone off, the day before, while Maigret was with the chief, wasn't that because the time he had allowed himself had run out, because he had to be back at the shop before a certain time? In that sort of establishment, the discipline is strict. Maigret knew this all the better in that in his early days he had spent nearly two years policing the big stores. He knew the atmosphere in them, the machinery, the rules and the intrigues.

At midday, he went back to the Boulevard Richard-Lenoir for lunch, and eventually noticed that it was the third day they were having grilled meat. He remembered in time about his wife's visit to Pardon. She must have been expecting him to express surprise at the new menus and no doubt she had got ready a more or less plausible explanation.

He avoided putting her in this predicament, and showed a certain tenderness towards her, perhaps a little too much, for she looked at him with a hint of anxiety in her eyes.

Of course, he was not thinking all the time about the trio in the Avenue de Châtillon. This affair only came back to him from time to time, in brief snatches, almost without his knowing it.

It was rather like a jigsaw puzzle and it irritated him in the way a puzzle does which you come back to in spite of yourself to try and fit a piece into place. The difference was that the pieces, in this case, were so to speak pieces of human beings.

Had he been unkind to Gisèle Marton, whose lip, when she had left him, had been trembling as if she had been going to cry?

It was possible. He had not done it on purpose. It was his job to try to find things out. In fact, he had taken rather a liking to her, as he had to the husband, too.

The two of them must have been in love when they were both working at the Magasins du Louvre, at the time when they had only two uncomfortable rooms over the workshop at their disposal.

Little by little, they had made improvements in their home. When the carpenter had left, they had extended their living-quarters by renting the ground floor, which, according to Janvier, had become an attractive room, and they had had an interior staircase put in so that they would not have to go outside to get from one floor to the next.

At present, they both had what is known as a good position, and they had bought a car.

There was a flaw somewhere, that was obvious. But where?

An idea came into his head and it was to come back to him several times. Marton's visit to Dr. Steiner worried him because, in the whole of his career, he could not remember coming across a man who had been to a neurologist or a psychiatrist to ask him:

'Do you think I am mad?'

His idea was that perhaps Marton had read, accidentally or otherwise, a treatise on psychiatry such as the one the chief-inspector had dipped into the night before.

At the same time as he was conjuring up the Avenue de Châtillon household in this way, Maigret took several telephone calls, saw a tradeswoman who had come to complain about a case of shop-lifting and sent her to see her local inspector, and went for a prowl round the inspectors' room where a dead calm still reigned.

Lapointe gave no sign of life and about five o'clock Maigret found himself back at his desk, lining up words in columns on the yellow jacket of a file.

First of all he had written: *frustration*.

Then, underneath: *inferiority complex*.

These were terms which he was not in the habit of using, and which he distrusted. Some years before, there had been an inspector who had come from university and who had only stayed a few months at the Quai. He was probably working in a legal bureau at present. He had read Freud, Adler and a few others and had been so deeply impressed by them that he claimed to be able to explain every case by psychoanalysis.

During his brief stay at Police Headquarters, he had been wrong every time and his colleagues had nicknamed him Inspector Complex.

The case of Xavier Marton was none the less an odd one in that it might have come straight out of the book which Maigret had read the day before and which he had finally closed in exasperation.

There were whole pages of the book dealing with frustration and its effects on the behaviour of the individual. Examples were given which might have been portraits of Marton.

A ward of the Board of Guardians, he had spent his childhood in a poverty-stricken farm in Sologne, with rough, brutish peasants who snatched his books out of his hands whenever they caught him reading.

He had none the less devoured every printed page he could get hold of, going from a popular novel to a scientific treatise, from mechanics to poetry, swallowing good and bad indiscriminately.

He had taken his first step forward by getting into a big store where, to begin with, only the humblest jobs had been entrusted to him.

One fact was characteristic. As soon as Marton could, he stopped living in more or less shabby furnished rooms, like most people starting their careers in Paris, and had his own flat instead. It only consisted of two rooms at the far end of a courtyard; the furniture was scanty, the comfort non-existent, but it was his home.

He went up in the world. Soon he could imagine that he was leading an orderly, middle-class life, and his first thought was, with his meagre means, to improve his living-quarters.

This was what Maigret put under the heading: inferiority complex. To be more precise, it was Marton's reaction against that complex.

The man needed to reassure himself. He also needed to show other people that he was not an inferior being, and he worked desperately hard to become an undisputed master in his field.

In his mind, didn't he consider himself rather as *King of the Electric Train?*

He was becoming somebody. He had become somebody. And, when he got married, it was to a girl of middle-class origins, a schoolmaster's daughter, who had her baccalaureate, and whose manners were different from those of the little salesgirls all around her.

Maigret, after some hesitation, wrote down a third word: *humiliation*.

His wife had outstripped him. She was now practically in business on her own account, in a luxury trade where every day she met famous women, high society, the rank and fashion of Paris. She was earning more than he was.

Certain phrases remained with Maigret from what he had read the day before. He could not remember them word for word but, in spite of himself, he tried to apply them to his problem.

One, for example, which said in substance that 'psychopaths shut themselves up in a world of their own, a dream-world which is more important to them than reality'. It was not quite that, but he was not going to make a fool of himself by going back to the chief's office for the book and consulting it all over again.

Besides, he did not really believe in it. All that stuff was just idle speculation.

But didn't electric trains, which were to be found not only in the Rue de Rivoli, but also in the studio in the Avenue de Châtillon, correspond fairly closely to this 'dream-world', to this 'shut-in world'?

Another passage reminded him of Xavier Marton's sang-froid, the conversation at the Quai des Orfèvres, the apparent logic of the way he had presented his case.

Maigret could no longer remember whether it was under the heading of neuroses, psychoses or paranoia, for the frontiers between these different domains did not seem to him to be very clearly defined.

'. . . *starting from false premises* . . .'

No. The text was different.

'. . . *on false or imaginary premises, the patient builds a closely reasoned argument, which is sometimes subtle and brilliant* . . .'

There was something similar about persecution mania, but here *'the patient starts from real facts, and draws conclusions from them which have an appearance of logic. . . .'*

The zinc phosphide was real. And in the Harris – Gisèle Marton, or rather Maurice Schwob – Gisèle Marton relationship, wasn't there something equivocal which was liable to affect the husband?

The most disturbing thing about this case was that, on closer examination, the young wife's behaviour, studied in the light of the same texts, produced an almost identical diagnosis.

She too was intelligent. She too discussed their case with apparent logic. She too . . .

'Oh, to blazes with it!'

Maigret looked for an india-rubber to erase the words he had written on the yellow file, filled his pipe, and went and planked himself down in front of the window, through which, in the darkness, he could see nothing but the dots of light that were the street-lamps.

When young Lapointe knocked at his door, half an hour later, he was dutifully filling in the blanks in an administrative questionnaire.

Lapointe had the advantage of coming from outside, from real life, and there remained a little fresh air in the folds of his overcoat, his nose was pink with cold and he was rubbing his hands together to warm them.

'I've done what you told me to, Chief.'

'He didn't smell a rat?'

'I don't think he noticed me.'

'Fire away.'

'First of all, I went up to the toy department and I bought the cheapest thing I could find, a little car that doesn't even go by clockwork. . . .'

He took it out of his pocket, and put it on the desk. It was canary yellow.

'A hundred and ten francs. I recognized Marton straight away from your description, but it was a woman who served me. Next, while I was waiting for the lunch-hour, I went and had a look at the Rue Saint-Honoré, without going in. The shop isn't far from the Place Vendôme. A narrow window, with practically nothing on display: a dressing-gown, a black silk slip and a pair of mules in gold-embroidered satin. On the glass, two words: "Harris, lingerie". Inside, it looks more like a drawing-room than a shop and you can tell it's a high-class firm.'

'Did you see her?'

'Yes. I'll come to that in a minute. It was time for me to go back to the Louvre, where I waited near the staff entrance. At midday, there's a regular stampede, like kids coming out of school, and everybody rushes off to the restaurants round about. Marton came out, in even more of a hurry than the others, and started walking very fast along the Rue du Louvre. He kept glancing all around him and he looked back two or three times, without paying any attention to me. At that time of day there's a lot of traffic and the pavements are crowded. . . .

'He turned left into the Rue Coquillière, where he hadn't gone more than a hundred yards before he went into a little restaurant called the "Trou Normand". The front is painted brown, with yellow letters, and the cyclostyled menu is stuck up on the left of the door.

'I hesitated and then decided to go in a few moments after him. It was full up. You could see that the people there were regulars and besides that, on one wall, there's a set of pigeon-holes where they keep the customers' napkins. I stopped at the bar and bought an *apéritif*.

' "Can I have lunch?"

'The manager, in a blue apron, looked into the dining-room, where there are only ten or so tables.

' "In a few minutes, there'll be a place for you. No. 3 has got to his cheese course."

'Marton was at the far end, by the kitchen door, sitting by himself in front of a paper table-cloth and a single cover. There was an empty place facing him. He said something to one of the two waitresses who seemed to know him and she laid a second cover.

'A few minutes went by. Marton, who had unfolded a newspaper, kept looking over it in the direction of the door.

'And soon, sure enough, a woman came in, spotted the table at the back straight away and went and sat down on the empty chair as if she was in the habit of doing this. They didn't kiss, they didn't shake hands. They just smiled at each other, and it seemed to me that their smiles were a little sad, or at least a little melancholy.'

'It wasn't his wife?' interrupted Maigret.

'No. I'd just seen his wife in the Rue Saint-Honoré and I'll come back to her later. From what you've told me, I should say it was the sister-in-law. The age and appearance tally. I don't know how to put it. . . .'

Well, well! Janvier, speaking about the same woman, had used almost exactly the same words.

'You get the impression of a real woman—I don't know if you understand what I mean—a woman who was born to love a man. Not to love in an ordinary way, but as men dream of being loved. . . .'

Maigret could not repress a smile on seeing Lapointe blush.

'I thought you were practically engaged?'

'I'm trying to explain to you the effect she must produce on most people. Sometimes, just like that, you meet a woman who starts you thinking straight away about . . .'

He could not find the right words any more.

'About what?'

'In spite of yourself you see her curling up in her companion's arms, you can almost feel her warmth. . . . At the same time you know that she's meant for one man alone, that she's a true mistress, an authentic lover. . . . After a while I got a place, two tables away from them, and that impression remained with me all through the meal . . . They didn't make the slightest suspicious gesture . . . They didn't hold hands . . . I don't think they even looked into each other's eyes . . . And yet . . .'

'You think they're in love?'

'I don't think they are. I'm certain of it. Even the waitress in her black dress and white apron, a great slatternly gawk of a girl, didn't serve them the way she served the other people and seemed to be making herself their accomplice. . . .'

'But you said at the beginning that they looked sad.'

'Let us say serious . . . I don't know, Chief . . . I'm sure they aren't unhappy, because you can't be really unhappy when you . . .'

Maigret smiled again as he wondered what would have been the report of a Lucas, for example, who would certainly not have had the same reactions as young Lapointe.

'Not unhappy, then, but sad, like lovers who aren't free to show their love . . .'

'If you like. At one point, he got up to help her off with her coat, because she'd glanced at the stove. It's a black woollen coat, with a bit of fur at the collar and the wrists. She was wearing a black dress too, in jersey, and I was surprised to see that she's rather on the plump side. . . .

'He looked at his watch several times. Then he asked the waitress to bring him his sweet and his coffee, while his companion had only got to roast veal.

'He got up while she was still eating, and, by way of leave-taking, he put his hand on her shoulder, in a gesture that was simple and tender at the same time.

'At the door he turned round. She smiled at him and he blinked his eyes. . . .

'I don't know if I did right to remain. I decided that he would be going back to the shop. I finished my dinner almost at the same time as the woman. Marton had paid the bill before going. I paid mine. I went out behind her and, without hurrying, she went and caught the Porte d'Orléans bus. I imagined she was going home to the Avenue de Châtillon and I didn't follow her. Did I do wrong?'

'You did right. And then?'

'I walked about a bit before going to the Rue Saint-Honoré, because the luxury shops scarcely ever open before two o'clock, and some of them not until half past two. I didn't want to arrive too early. I must admit too that I was a bit windy. Apart from that, I wanted to see the boss and I said to myself that he's probably the sort who lunches in the big restaurants and isn't in any hurry.'

Maigret was looking at Lapointe with almost fatherly benevolence, for he had taken him under his wing when, two years earlier, the young man had come to the Quai des Orfèvres, where he had made remarkable progress.

87

'I'll tell you something, Chief. I was so scared at the idea of going into a shop like that that first of all I treated myself to a *calvados*.'

'Go on.'

'The first time I had almost pushed open the glass door when I saw two old ladies in mink coats sitting in the armchairs, facing the saleswoman, and I didn't dare. I waited till they came out. A Rolls with a chauffeur was waiting for them a little way off.

'Then, for fear another customer might arrive, I rushed in.

'At first, I didn't look at anything around me, I was so nervous.

' "I want a nightdress for a young lady," I said.

'I supposed it was Madame Marton who stood before me. Besides, when, a little later, I looked at her, I noticed that she had certain features in common with the young woman at the "Trou Normand". Madame Marton is a little taller, with a good figure too, but her body looks harder, what they call a statuesque figure. You see what I mean?

' "What sort of nightdress?" she asked me. "Please sit down. . . ."

'Because it isn't the kind of shop where you stay on your feet. I told you it looks like a drawing-room. At the back, there are curtains hiding some cubicles which must be used for trying on, and I noticed, in one of them, a big mirror and a cane stool.

' "What is the young lady's size?"

' "She's a bit shorter than you, and not so broad across the shoulders. . . ."

'I don't think she smelt a rat. She looked at me all the time in a patronizing sort of way and I felt that she was thinking I must have come to the wrong shop.

' "We have this one, in real silk, with hand-made lace. I suppose it's for a present?"

'I stammered that it was.

' "This is the model we created for the trousseau of Princess Helen of Greece."

'I was determined to stay as long as possible. I said hesitantly:

' "I suppose it's very dear?"

' "Forty-five thousand . . . It's a 40 . . . If the young lady's size is different, we shall have to make it to measure, for this is the only one we have in stock . . ."

' "You haven't something less exotic? In nylon, for instance? . . ." '

Maigret remarked:

'I say, Lapointe, you seem to know all about it. I thought it wasn't done to buy lingerie for a fiancée.'

'I had to play the game properly. At the word "nylon", she took on a scornful, supercilious expression.

' "We don't stock nylon here. Only pure silk and batiste . . ."

'The door opened. It was in the mirror, to begin with, that I saw a man in a camel-hair coat to whom, straight away, the saleswoman gave a wink. I imagine, Chief, that that meant she had a queer customer on her hands.

'The man took his hat and coat off, and went behind the counter into a narrow office where he hung his things on a coat-stand. He left a whiff of perfume behind him. I could see him bending over some papers which he was glancing at casually.

'Then he came back into the shop where, looking at his fingernails, then at us in turn, like someone who is completely at home, he seemed to be patiently waiting for me to make up my mind.

'I asked at a venture:

' "What have you got in white? I'd like something very simple, without any lace. . . ."

'They exchanged another glance and the woman bent down to take a box out of a drawer.

'Monsieur Harris, or Schwob, is the sort of man you meet around the Place Vendôme and the Champs-Elysées, and he might just as easily be in the cinema trade as in exports, pictures or antiques. You know what I mean, don't you? He must go to his barber's every morning and have a facial massage. His suit is beautifully cut, without a single crease, and he certainly doesn't buy his shoes ready-made.

'He has dark hair, with a touch of silver at the temples, a clean-shaven face, a matt complexion, a distant and sardonic gaze.

' "This is the least expensive thing we have . . ."

'A nightdress that looked nothing at all, with just a few stitches of embroidery.

' "How much?"

' "Eighteen thousand."

'Another glance between them.

' "I suppose it isn't what you're looking for?"

'And already she was opening the box to put the nightdress back.

' "I'll have to think about it . . . I'll come back. . . ."

' "Yes, do."

'I nearly forgot my hat on the counter and had to go back for it. Once I was outside, and the door shut, I turned round and saw the two of them laughing.

'I walked about a hundred yards, then I came past on the opposite pavement. There was nobody left in the shop. The curtain of the little office was open, the woman sitting there, and Harris busy, in front of a mirror, running a comb through his hair. . . .

'That's all, Chief. I can't swear that they sleep together. What is certain is that they make a good pair and they don't need to speak to understand each other. You can tell that straight away.

'Madame Marton doesn't lunch with her husband although they work a quarter of a mile from each other, and it was the sister-in-law who went to meet Xavier Marton.

'Finally, I imagine that these two have to keep their meetings secret. Marton, in fact, has very little time at his disposal for his midday meal.

Close to the Magasins du Louvre, there are lots of cheap restaurants which I saw the salesmen and saleswomen dashing into.

'But he takes the trouble to go quite a distance, to a restaurant with a different clientele where no one would think of looking for him.

'Is Madame Marton in the habit of lunching with Monsieur Harris? I just don't know. The fact that he arrived at the shop after her doesn't prove anything.'

Maigret got up to regulate the radiator which, as on the day before, was showing a tendency to get out of hand. All day long, they had been expecting snow, which was forecast and was already covering the North and Normandy.

Hadn't the chief-inspector been right to send the treatises on psychiatry and all those stories of psychoses and complexes to the devil?

He had, at last, the impression of finding himself face to face with people of flesh and blood, men and women with their passions and their interests.

Yesterday, it had just been a question of a couple of people.

Today there seemed to be two couples and that made a tremendous difference.

'Where are you sending me now?' asked Lapointe, who in his turn was becoming passionately interested in the case and was afraid of being taken off it.

'You can't go to the Rue Saint-Honoré any more, or to the Avenue de Châtillon, now that the two women have seen you. . . .'

Besides, what could he have gone and done there? It was the Public Prosecutor who appeared to be in the right. Nothing had happened. Probably nothing would. Unless one of the two couples, growing impatient. . . .

Just at that moment the telephone rang, Maigret looked at the black marble clock which was always ten minutes fast. It said twenty to six.

'Inspector Maigret, yes . . .'

Why did he feel a slight shock on recognizing the voice? Was it because, ever since the morning before, his only thoughts had been about the man at the other end of the line?

There were noises and voices in the background. Maigret could have sworn that his caller, full of anxiety, was holding his hand cupped in front of his mouth. He was speaking in a low voice.

'I must apologize about yesterday, but I was forced to go. All I want to know is whether you will still be at your office about a quarter to seven, or perhaps ten to seven. We close at half past six . . .'

'Today?'

'If you don't mind . . .'

'I'll be expecting you.'

Marton rang off straight away, after stammering a thank-you, and Maigret looked at Lapointe rather as Madame Marton and Monsieur Harris looked at one another in the lingerie shop.

'It's him?'

'Yes.'

'He's coming here?'

'In an hour and a quarter.'

Maigret felt tempted to laugh at himself, and at all the ideas he had thought up about a case which, in an hour and a quarter, would no doubt appear perfectly simple to him.

'We've time to go and have a pint at the Brasserie Dauphine,' he growled, opening his cupboard to take his hat and coat.

5

It was just as he was going downstairs with Lapointe that the idea struck Maigret.

'I'll be with you in a minute. Wait for me.'

And, still hesitating, he made for the inspectors' office. His idea was for one of his men to start shadowing Xavier Marton at the entrance to the Magasins du Louvre. He did not know precisely why, in fact. Or rather, he felt that several things might happen. To begin with, Marton was capable of changing his mind at the last moment, as had happened a first time when he had left Maigret's office during the latter's absence. Or else his wife, who admitted having followed him the previous day, might well shadow him again.

If she accosted him in the street, wouldn't he accompany her to the Avenue de Châtillon? There were other possibilities too. And, even if nothing happened, Maigret would not be sorry to find out how the electric-train salesman behaved while taking this important step, whether he hesitated, whether he stopped on the way, for example, to steel himself by drinking a glass or two.

Janvier risked being recognized. Another inspector working on his own, Lucas, for instance, who was free, but who had never seen Marton, might not be able to recognize him, from his description, among all the staff coming out.

'Lucas and Janvier! Cut along, both of you, to the Magasins du Louvre. When the staff come out, don't show your face, Janvier, but just point out Marton as he goes by and you, Lucas, will do the shadowing alone.'

Lucas, who did not know much about the case, asked:

'Do you think it will be a long job, that he'll go very far?'

'Here, probably.'

He nearly added:

'Above all, no taxis, no expenses!'

For there are certain administrative rules of which the public knows nothing but which, for the men of Police Headquarters, are sometimes of great importance. When a crime, or an offence, is committed, and when the police, in consequence, make investigations on the basis of powers delegated by the judiciary, the professional expenses of the chief-inspectors, inspectors and technicians are as a rule chargeable to the culprit. If he is not arrested, or if the courts later find him not guilty, the Ministry of Justice foots the bill.

If on the other hand it is a case which Police Headquarters are investigating on their own initiative and if, in the end, there is neither crime nor culprit, then the bill for expenses is charged to the Prefecture, that is to say to the Ministry of the Interior.

Now, for the police, this makes an enormous difference. The Ministry of Justice, which always thinks that the criminal will pay, is not too close-fisted and does not make a fuss about a taxi more or less. The Prefecture, on the contrary, scrutinizes every bill, demanding an account of the most trifling comings and goings which cost the treasury anything.

In the present affair, wasn't Maigret working to ensure that there was neither a crime nor a culprit?

This meant therefore no bill for expenses, or a bill which was as modest as possible, and he knew that, if nothing happened, he would have to justify the use of his men.

'Let's go!'

There was no snow, as the radio had forecast, but a cold, yellowish fog. The two men, in the heat and light of the Brasserie Dauphine, did not order beers, which seemed unseasonable, but *apéritifs*. Elbows on the bar, they said nothing about Marton, chatted a little with the *patron*, and then, with their coat-collars turned up, went back to the Quai.

Maigret had decided to leave the door of the

inspectors' office slightly ajar and behind that door to install Lapointe who was a fairly good shorthand writer. It was a precaution, just in case.

At ten to seven, he was sitting at his desk, waiting for old Joseph to knock at the door. At five to seven, he was still waiting and Lapointe, with a well-sharpened pencil in his hand, was also waiting behind the door.

The chief-inspector was beginning to lose patience when, at one minute to seven, he finally heard footsteps, a familiar little knock, and saw the white porcelain handle turning.

It was Joseph. Notified beforehand, he contented himself with murmuring:

'It's the gentleman you're expecting.'

'Show him in.'

'Forgive me for being a little late,' said Marton. 'It was useless for me to take the Metro at this time of day. Two buses were full and so I came on foot, thinking it would be quicker. . . .'

He was panting slightly, and looked hot from running.

'If you want to take your coat off . . .'

'Perhaps it would be a good idea. I think I'm starting a cold. . . .'

Settling down took some time. He did not know where to put his overcoat. First he put it on a chair, noticed that it was the one where he ought to sit to face the chief-inspector, and carried it to the other end of the room.

At last, they were sitting together in conversation, Maigret smoking his pipe and studying his caller more closely than on the day before. He was almost disappointed. For twenty-four hours, his thoughts had been revolving round Marton, who had ended up by becoming an extraordinary figure, and now all he had before him was an ordinary little man, such as you rub shoulders with by the hundred in the Metro or in the street.

He was a little vexed with him for being so commonplace, for behaving in such a normal way.

'I must apologize again for leaving your office without telling you. At the shop, discipline is strict. I had obtained permission to be away for an hour to go and see my dentist, who lives in the Rue Saint-Roch, a stone's throw from the Louvre. Here I suddenly noticed that time was passing and I had to be at my post at eleven to take delivery of some goods. I meant to leave a message with your porter, the old man who showed me in, but he wasn't in the corridor. I ought to have rung you up, but we are forbidden to make private calls and most of the telephones are connected to the switchboard.'

'How did you manage this afternoon?'

'To ring you up, I took advantage of the fact that there wasn't anybody in the floor manager's office, where there's an outside telephone. You'll have noticed that I was quick about saying what I had to say to you and that I rang off in a hurry. . . .'

There was nothing extraordinary in all that. But the chief-inspector insisted:

'At midday, when you went to lunch . . .'

'In the first place, I said to myself that you'd be out at lunch too. And then, it seemed to me that you didn't regard my business as very serious . . .'

'And is it serious?'

'Certainly. It was you who sent somebody to prowl round my department, wasn't it?'

Maigret did not answer. The other continued:

'You won't admit it, but I'm sure that it was a detective.'

He must have prepared this conversation as he had prepared the first. There were however some moments of hesitation, like gaps. He hesitated for quite a while before asking:

'My wife has been to see you, hasn't she?'

'What makes you think that?'

'I don't know. I've known her a long time. I'm sure she suspects something. Women have antennae. And, with her character, if she senses the slightest danger, she'll attack. You understand what I'm getting at?'

A silence, during which he looked at Maigret reproachfully, as if he were vexed with him for not playing fair with him.

'Has she been?'

The chief-inspector hesitated in his turn, realizing that it was a heavy responsibility to take on. If Marton was, to any extent, mentally ill, the answer could have a capital influence on his future behaviour.

A little earlier, alone in his office, Maigret had nearly telephoned his friend Pardon to ask him to be present at the interview. But hadn't the doctor already told him that he knew next to nothing about psychiatry?

Xavier Marton was there, in his chair, three feet away from the chief-inspector, talking and gesticulating like any other caller. Perhaps he was a normal man, who felt that his life was in danger and had honestly come to tell the police all about it.

Perhaps too he was a neurotic, suffering from persecution mania, who needed reassurance.

Perhaps he was a lunatic.

And finally, perhaps he was a man tormented by diabolical ideas, a madman too, in a certain sense, but a lucid, intelligent madman, who had drawn up a detailed plan which he intended to carry out at all costs.

His face was very ordinary. He had a nose, a mouth, eyes and ears like everybody else. The blood had gone to his head, as a result of the contrast between the cold outside and the heat of the office, and perhaps that was what was making his eyes shine, or else it was the cold in the head of which he had spoken.

Was he really starting a cold in the head or had he just mentioned it because he knew that his eyes were going to shine?

Maigret felt ill at ease. He began to suspect that the man had only come back in order to ask the question about his wife.

Had he in his turn spied on her? Did he know

that she had been to the Quai des Orfèvres and did he hope to find out what she had said?

'She has been here,' the chief-inspector finally admitted.

'What did she tell you?'

'Here, as a rule, people answer questions, they don't ask them.'

'I beg your pardon.'

'Your wife is very elegant, Monsieur Marton.'

He gave a mechanical twitch of the lips which did duty for a smile and which was not without irony, or bitterness.

'I know. She has always dreamt of being elegant. She decided to be elegant.'

He had stressed the word *decided* as, in a letter, he would have underlined it, and Maigret remembered that it had happened before that his caller had emphasized a word.

Hadn't he read, in the treatise on psychiatry, that insistently underlining words was a sign of . . . ?

But he refused to put the interview on that particular plane.

'Yesterday morning, you came and told me that you were afraid for your life. You spoke to me about the attitude your wife had adopted for some time, and of a poisonous chemical which you had found in a cupboard. You also told me that several times, after a meal, you had felt ill. At that point, I was called to see the Director and our conversation did not continue later, for you had gone. I suppose you had some other details to give me?'

Marton gave the rather melancholy smile of a man who is being treated unjustly.

'There's a way of asking questions which makes it difficult to answer them,' he observed.

Maigret nearly lost his temper, for it seemed that he was being taught a lesson and he was aware that he deserved it.

'But, dammit all, you aren't going to tell me that you came here without any definite object? Are you lodging a complaint against your wife?'

Marton shook his head.

'You aren't accusing her?'

'What of?' he asked.

'If what you've told me is true, you can accuse her of attempted murder.'

'Do you really think that that would result in anything? What proof have I got? You yourself don't believe me. I've given you a sample of zinc phosphide, but I might just as well have put it in the broom-cupboard myself. From the fact that I went, of my own accord, to see a neurologist, it will be assumed that I'm not entirely sane, or else—and this would be just as plausible—that I'm trying to create that impression.'

It was the first time that Maigret had had a customer like this before him and he could not help staring at him in amazement.

Every reply, every new attitude baffled him. He kept hunting in vain for a flaw, a weak point, and, without fail, it was he himself who was put in his place.

'My wife is sure to have spoken to you about my neurasthenia. She will have told you too that, in the evening, when I'm pottering about, I'll often stamp my feet and actually burst into tears because I can't do something I have in mind . . .'

'You've mentioned this to Dr. Steiner?'

'I told him everything. For a whole hour, he asked me questions that you would never dream of asking.'

'Well?'

He looked Maigret in the eyes.

'Well, I'm not mad.'

'And you're still convinced that your wife intends to kill you?'

'Yes.'

'But you don't want us to start inquiries?'

'That wouldn't do any good.'

'Or to protect you?'

'How?'

'Then, once again, why did you come here?'

'So that you would know. So that, if anything happened to me, you wouldn't think it was death from natural causes, as would be the case if you hadn't been told. I've read a lot about poisonings. According to your own experts, you have to reckon nine cases of criminal poisoning that are unknown, and therefore unpunished, to one case where the culprit is discovered.'

'Where did you read that?'

'In a scientific detection review.'

'You take it regularly?'

'No. I read it in a public library. Now, I can tell you one last thing: I don't intend to go quietly.'

Maigret gave a slight start, feeling that at last they were coming to the heart of the matter.

'What exactly do you mean?'

'First of all, that I'm taking precautions, as I told you yesterday. And then that, precisely because of the statistics I've just quoted, I'm not going to rely on the law and, if I have enough time, I'll mete out justice myself.'

'Am I to understand that you are going to kill your wife *in advance*?'

'Before dying, of course, but not before she has succeeded in poisoning me. There are very few poisons which can cause instantaneous death and they are nearly all extremely difficult to get hold of. Therefore there will be a certain lapse of time between the moment I shall know she has succeeded and the moment I shall be incapable of action. I have a loaded revolver at home. I should add that it is properly licensed, as you can find out from the town hall. My wife knows about it, because I've had it for years. Only, for some time now, it has been hidden somewhere where she won't find it. She has been looking for it. She's still looking . . .'

There were moments when Maigret asked himself whether he wouldn't be well advised to take the man, straight away, to the special infirmary at the *Dépôt*.

'Suppose that tonight, half an hour after dinner, you feel a pain in the stomach?'

'Don't worry, Monsieur Maigret. I'm capable of telling the difference between poisoning and ordinary indigestion. Apart from that, I've always had an excellent stomach.'

'But if you think that you've been poisoned, you'll act?'

'If I *feel* that I've been poisoned, I shan't hesitate.'

'You'll shoot?'

'Yes.'

The telephone started ringing and it seemed to the chief-inspector that it was making an unusual din in the room, where the atmosphere had finally become oppressive, tense, almost unhealthy . . .

'It's Lucas, Chief.'

'Yes . . .'

'I couldn't let you know any sooner, because I didn't want to leave her alone on the embankment . . .'

'Who?'

'The woman . . . I'll explain in a minute . . . I had to wait until an inspector passed near me before I could hand over to him and come up here to phone you . . . It's Torrence who's taken my place . . .'

'Be quick about it. Don't talk too loud, because you're making the receiver vibrate . . .'

Had Marton realized that all this concerned him indirectly?

'I understand, Chief . . . Here goes! . . . Janvier showed me your man as he was coming out of the shop . . . I started following him, by myself, while Janvier waited for a bus . . .'

'And then?'

'As long as we were walking through the crowds, which are dense at this time of day, I didn't notice anything. But, crossing the court-yard of the Louvre, and then getting on to the embankment, I realized that I wasn't the only one who was following him . . .'

'Go on.'

'There was a woman close on his heels . . . I don't think she noticed me, but I can't be sure . . . She followed him as far as the Quai des Orfèvres and she's still there, about a hundred yards from the entrance . . .'

'Describe . . .'

'It isn't worth it. When Torrence came near me and I'd handed over to him, I came up here and asked Janvier to go and have a look down below, seeing that he's been on the case . . . He's just come back and he's beside me now . . . Would you like to have a word with him?'

'Yes.'

'Hullo, Chief . . . It's the sister-in-law, Jenny . . .'

'You're sure?'

'Certain.'

'She didn't recognize you?'

'No. I took precautions.'

'Thanks.'

'No instructions?'

'Torrence is to go on watching her.'

'And what about the man? Has Lucas to keep on following him when he comes out?'

'Yes.'

He rang off, and found Marton's inquiring gaze fixed on him.

'Is it my wife?' asked the electric-train enthusiast.

'What do you mean?'

'Nothing. I should have known that you wouldn't tell me the truth anyway.'

'You heard?'

'No. Only, it isn't difficult to understand, from the little you said yourself. If it is my wife . . .'

'Well? What then?'

'Nothing. I was wrong to come and see you yesterday, and even more so to come back today. Seeing that you don't believe me . . .'

'I ask nothing better than to believe you. Why, look here! Since you're so sure of yourself, I'll make you a proposal. Dr. Steiner, restrained by his professional oath of secrecy, won't tell me anything.'

'You want me to submit to an examination by another doctor?'

'By the specialist at the special infirmary at the *Dépôt*. He's a trustworthy man, a professor known all over the world.'

'When? Straight away?'

Was Maigret wrong? Was there, in his caller, a moment of panic?

'No. At this hour, I can't possibly bother him. He'll be in his department tomorrow morning.'

Calmly, Marton replied:

'If it isn't too early, I'll have time to tell the shop.'

'You agree to it?'

'Why shouldn't I agree to it?'

'You also agree to sign a paper for me stating that it's of your own free will that you're having this examination?'

'If you insist.'

'You're a curious fellow, Monsieur Marton.'

'You think so?'

'You are here of your own free will too, I'm not forgetting that. You aren't obliged to answer my questions. However, there are a few I should like to ask you.'

'Will you believe me?'

'I shall try, and I can assure you that I'm not prejudiced against you in any way.'

This declaration only called forth a disabused smile.

'Do you love your wife?'

'Now?'

'Now, of course.'

'In that case, no.'

'Does she love you?'

'She hates me.'

'That isn't the impression I'd got of the couple you form when you left here yesterday morning.'

'We didn't have time to go to the root of the matter, and you didn't want to anyway.'

'Just as you like. Shall I go on?'

'Do, please.'

'Did you ever love her?'

'I thought I did.'

'Explain to me what you mean by that.'

'Till then, I'd lived on my own, without allowing myself the slightest distraction. I've worked hard, you know. Starting as low as I did, I had to make a tremendous effort to become what I have become.'

'You'd never had anything to do with women before you met your wife?'

'Rarely. The sort of adventure you can imagine. It left me with more shame than pleasure. So that, when I met Gisèle, I saw her as the ideal woman and it was that ideal woman that I loved. At that time the word *couple* was a marvellous word to me. I dreamt about it. We were going to be a couple. I was going to become one of the halves of a couple. I wouldn't be alone any more at home, in life. And, one day, we would have children . . .'

'You haven't any?'

'Gisèle doesn't want any.'

'Had she told you beforehand?'

'No. If she had told me, I'd have married her all the same and I'd have been satisfied with just the couple . . .'

'Did she love you?'

'I thought so.'

'You realized one day that you'd been mistaken?'

'Yes.'

'When?'

He did not reply straight away. He seemed to have found himself faced with a serious matter of conscience and he was thinking. Maigret, for his part, did not hustle him.

'I suppose,' Marton murmured at last, 'that you've made inquiries. If you sent somebody to spy on me at the shop, you must have sent one of your men too to the Avenue de Châtillon.'

'That's correct.'

'In that case, I'd better speak frankly. To the question you've just asked me, I answer: Two years ago.'

'In other words, it was about the time your sister-in-law came to live with you both that you realized that your wife didn't love you and that she had never loved you?'

'Yes.'

'Can you explain to me why?'

'That's easy. Before knowing my sister-in-law, who was living in America with her husband, I wasn't always happy at home, but I used to tell myself that I was as happy as anyone could be. You understand? In other words, I considered my disappointments to be unavoidable, imagining that other men were all in the same boat. In short, Gisèle was a woman and I'd come to believe that her faults were the faults inherent in every woman.'

He was still searching for his words, pronouncing some with greater emphasis than others.

'Like everybody else, I suppose, I'd dreamt of a certain form of love, of union, of fusion, call it what you will, and, after a few years or a few months, I'd come to the conclusion that it doesn't exist.'

'You mean, that love doesn't exist.'

'That sort of love, at least.'

111

'What is it that you hold against your wife?'

'What you're making me do probably isn't in very good taste, but if I don't answer you truthfully, you'll go and draw the wrong conclusions again. I know now, for instance, that, if Gisèle left Rouen and her family, it was just out of ambition. Not out of love for the man she followed at that time and who dropped her after a few months, as she would like people to think. That man, he was the first rung of the ladder, he was Paris. Even if he hadn't left her, she wouldn't have stayed with him for long.'

It was strange to hear him talking like this, coolly, dispassionately, as if he were studying an impersonal case, and trying to be clear and precise.

'Only, she imagined that things would move faster than they did. She was young, pretty, desirable. She didn't expect to go running from one waiting-room to the next and copying out advertisements of situations vacant from the windows of newspaper offices just to finish up in the lingerie department of a big store.'

'You aren't ambitious yourself, I suppose?'

'It isn't the same. Let me finish with her. She went out in the evenings with colleagues, mostly heads of departments, but either they were married, or else they didn't propose to her. It was at that moment, just as she felt that she was growing old, that I came on the scene. Three or four years earlier, she would have laughed at me. Experience had shown her that I was an acceptable last resource and she did what was necessary.'

'That is to say?'

'She allowed me to believe that she loved me. For years, I thought of nothing but the couple we formed, of what I called our nest, of what I also called our future. I found her cold, but I consoled myself with the thought that women who aren't are putting on an act. I found her selfish, even avaricious, and promptly persuaded myself that women are all like that.'

'You were unhappy?'

'I had my work. She poked fun at it, called me a maniac, was ashamed, I know that now, to be married to a man whose job was children's toys and electric trains. She had found something better.'

Maigret could tell what was coming.

'What do you mean?'

'She made the acquaintance of a man who worked for some time at the shop, a certain Maurice Schwob. I don't know whether she loves him. It's possible. At least, he has helped her to take another step forward, and a big step at that. He's married to a former actress who was kept for a long time and who has a lot of money . . .'

'Is that why your wife hasn't asked for a divorce in order to marry Schwob?'

'I suppose so. The fact remains that they've opened a shop together with the old woman's money.'

'You think they are lovers?'

'I know they are.'

'You've followed them?'

'I'm as inquisitive as the next man.'

'But you haven't asked for a divorce yourself?'

He did not reply. They seemed to have come to a dead end.

'This situation already existed before your sister-in-law's arrival?'

'That is probably so, but my eyes weren't open yet.'

'You told me just now that it's since your sister-in-law has been living with you in the Avenue de Châtillon that you've understood. What have you understood?'

'That there are other sorts of women, of women such as those I'd always dreamt of.'

'You love her?'

'Yes.'

'She's your mistress?'

'No.'

'Yet you sometimes meet each other unknown to your wife?'

'You know that too?'

'I know the little restaurant called the "Trou Normand".'

'That's correct. Jenny often comes and joins me at lunch-time. My wife, for her part, nearly always goes with Schwob to more expensive places. She no longer belongs to our world, you understand?'

This last word kept cropping up, as if Marton were afraid that Maigret was incapable of following him.

'You understand?'

'Does your sister-in-law love you too?'

'I think she's beginning to.'

'She's just beginning?'

'She was really in love with her husband. They formed a real couple, those two. They lived in New Jersey, not far from New York, in a pretty country house. Edgar was killed in an accident and Jenny tried to commit suicide. She turned on the gas, one evening, and was saved only just in time. Then, not knowing what to do any more, she came back to Europe and we took her in. She was still in deep mourning. Gisèle pokes fun at her, and advises her to go out and enjoy herself, to change her ideas. I, on the other hand, am gently trying to give her back a taste for life. . . .'

'Have you succeeded?'

He blushed like an adolescent.

'I think so. You understand now why she isn't my mistress? I love her and I respect her. I wouldn't want, for the sake of selfish satisfaction . . .'

Was Lapointe taking all this down in shorthand? If this interrogation went through the ordinary administrative channels, it was probably Maigret who would look silly.

'Does Jenny know that her sister wants you out of the way?'

'I haven't spoken to her about it.'

'She knows that you don't get on together?'

'She's living with us. I ought to point out that we never quarrel, my wife and I. On the surface,

115

we lead the same life as any other couple. Gisèle is too intelligent to provoke any quarrels. And then there are ten million francs to be picked up, which would allow her to have an equal share in the Rue Saint-Honoré business, with this Schwob who calls himself Harris.'

'What ten million francs?'

'The insurance money.'

'When did you take out an insurance policy? Before or after your sister-in-law's arrival?'

'Before. It was about four years ago. Gisèle was already working with Schwob. An insurance agent came to see us, apparently by chance, but I realized later that it was my wife who'd asked him to call. You know how it goes. "You don't know who's going to live or who's going to die," he said. "It's a comfort to the one who's going to know that the one who remains . . ." '

He laughed, for the first time, a short unpleasant laugh.

'I was still very ignorant. To cut a long story short, we ended up by signing a policy for ten million.'

'You say *we?*'

'Yes, because it's a joint life policy, as they call it.'

'In other words, if your wife happens to die you collect ten million too?'

'Certainly.'

'So that you have as much interest in her death as she has in yours?'

'I make no secret of the fact.'

'And you hate each other?'

'She hates me, yes.'

'And you?'

'I don't hate her. I'm just taking precautions.'

'But you love your sister-in-law.'

'I make no secret of that, either.'

'And your wife is Schwob-Harris's mistress.'

'That's a fact.'

'Have you anything else to tell me?'

'I can't think of anything. I've answered all your questions. I think I've even anticipated some of them. I'm ready to submit, tomorrow morning, to the examination you've told me about. What time do I have to be here?'

'Between ten o'clock and midday. What time would suit you best?'

'Will it take long?'

'About as long as at Dr. Steiner's.'

'That means an hour. Let's say eleven o'clock, if that's all right with you, because that way I won't need to go back to the shop.'

He got up, hesitantly, perhaps expecting some more questions. While he was putting on his overcoat, Maigret murmured:

'Your sister-in-law is waiting for you on the embankment.'

He stayed for a moment with one arm in the air, the sleeve half on.

'Oh!'

'Does that surprise you? Didn't she know you were coming here?'

There was a second's hesitation, but it did not escape Maigret's notice.

'Of course she didn't.'

This time, he was lying, that was obvious. He was suddenly in a hurry to get away. He was not so sure of himself any more.

'Good-bye till tomorrow,' he stammered.

And, as he had automatically begun to put out his hand, he had to go through with it. Maigret shook hands with him, watched him making for the stairs, and shut the door, standing stock-still behind it for a good few moments and breathing hard.

'Whew!' he sighed as Lapointe, his wrist aching, appeared in the other doorway.

He could not remember an interrogation as astonishing as this had been.

6

'LUCAS?' asked Maigret, with a jerk of the head towards the communicating door between the two offices.

Not only did Lapointe grasp the meaning of the question, but he also understood that just then the chief-inspector had no desire to talk a lot.

'He's gone back to take Torrence's place on the embankment. As Torrence wasn't in the picture . . .'

Suddenly, Maigret went straight from one idea to another and, once again, the inspector followed him without difficulty.

'What do you think about it?'

Except with Janvier, to whom he had always spoken familiarly, Maigret only used the *tu* form of address—and then only with a few people— in the heat of action, or else when he was very worried. It always gave pleasure to Lapointe, for, when it happened, it was rather as if the two men had suddenly confided secrets to each other.

'I don't know, Chief. I heard him without seeing him, which is rather different. . . .'

That was precisely why the chief-inspector was asking for his opinion. They had heard the same words. But the young man, behind the door, had not been distracted by a face, eyes and hands on which his attention was dispersed. He was rather in the position of the attendants, at the theatre, who hear the play from the corridors and for whom the tirades being declaimed have a different resonance.

'He gave me the impression of being an honest man.'

'Not rather mad?'

'It must be difficult to explain oneself, faced with somebody like you . . .'

Lapointe had hesitated about saying that, for fear of being misunderstood, when in his eyes it was a compliment.

'You'll see what I mean better when you read your side of the interview. It was only at the end . . .'

'What, at the end?'

'That he was probably lying. At least in my opinion. The sister-in-law must have known that he was coming here. He knew that she knew. What he didn't know was that she'd followed him and that she was waiting for him on the embankment. I think that made him angry. You want me to type the text out straight away?'

Maigret shook his head, adding:

'I hope that you won't need to type it out.'

He was beginning to grow impatient, wondering why Lucas had not come back. There was no point in following the couple to the Avenue de Châtillon. The chief-inspector was eager to know how the reunion had gone and Lapointe shared his curiosity.

'I wonder,' murmured the inspector, 'why he said that his sister-in-law wasn't in the know.'

'He could have had a reason.'

'What reason?'

'A desire to avoid compromising her, to make sure that she couldn't be accused one day of complicity.'

'She couldn't be unless . . .'

Lapointe broke off, and threw a look of surprise at his chief. Maigret's words implied that something was going to happen, something which would put Xavier Marton in a difficult position. He had no time to say any more on the subject, for some quick, rather short footsteps were heard which could only be Lucas's. The latter came through the inspectors' office, and appeared framed in the half-open doorway.

'Can I come in, Chief?'

He was still wearing his overcoat, a black overcoat, in a shaggy material on which there could still be seen a few small white specks.

'It's snowing?'

'It's beginning. Fine snow, but heavy.'

'Fire away.'

'The poor kid, on the embankment, couldn't have been any warmer than I was, especially as she's wearing light shoes, and I could hear her heels tapping on the pavement. First of all, she stood still by the stone parapet, avoiding the lamps. From the way she was standing, I could guess, although I only saw her silhouette, that she was looking at the lighted windows. There aren't many left in the building. I saw them too, going out one after the other. From time to time, you could hear voices under the archway. I'd never realized before that our voices, when we go out, carry so far. Inspectors, in groups of two or three came out, wished each other good night, and separated . . .

'She gradually drew nearer, as if the lights in your office fascinated her, and she became more and more nervous. I'm sure that several times she was on the point of crossing the road and coming in . . .'

'She must have thought I'd arrested him?'

'I don't know. Finally he came out, all alone, and walked past the policeman on duty. Straight away, he peered around him, as if he were looking for somebody. . . .'

'He was looking for her. I'd just told him that she was there.'

'Now I understand. It was difficult for him to see her where she was. First of all he looked for her towards the Pont-Neuf, but she was standing in the opposite direction. He came back. I thought she was going to take advantage of the moment he had his back turned to slip away, or to go down on to the loading quay, but he found her before she could move. I couldn't hear what they said. From their attitudes, I got the impression that he began by reproving her. He wasn't gesticulating but his attitude was that of an angry man.

'It was she who slipped her hand under his arm, pointing out the duty policeman to him, and pulled him away towards the Pont Saint-Michel . . .'

'One moment,' Maigret broke in. 'How did she put her hand under his arm?'

If Lucas did not appear to see the purport of this question, Lapointe, who was in love, did.

'In a normal way, like any woman you see in the street with her lover or her husband. He must have reproached her some more, not so energetically. Then I suppose he noticed she was cold and he put his arm round her waist. Their bodies came a little closer together. They began walking in step, at the same pace . . .'

Lapointe and Maigret looked at each other, thinking the same thing.

'When they got to the Pont Saint-Michel, they hesitated and then, crossing the line of cars, still holding each other round the waist, they went into the bar on the corner. There were a lot of people round the counter. It's *apéritif* time. I could see them through the steamy windowpanes. I didn't go in. They were both standing near the cash-desk. The barman prepared a hot toddy and put it on the counter in front of the young woman, who seemed to be protesting. Marton insisted. Finally she drank the toddy, blowing on it, while he just had a coffee.'

'Now I come to think of it,' Maigret said to Lapointe, 'what did he drink at midday in the restaurant?'

'Mineral water.'

It was curious. If anybody had asked him, Maigret would in fact have sworn that the electric-train enthusiast drank neither wine nor spirits.

'When they came out,' concluded Lucas 'they made for the bus stop and waited there. I saw them get on the bus. They were going in the direction of the Porte d'Orléans and I thought it best to come and report to you. Did I do right?'

Maigret nodded. The snow had disappeared from Lucas's overcoat. During this conversation, he had been warming his hands on the radiator.

The chief-inspector used the familiar *tu* with him as well.

'Have you anything fixed for this evening?'

'Nothing special.'

'Nor have I,' said Lapointe quickly.

'I don't know which of the two of you I'm going to ask to spend the night outside. In this weather, it won't be very pleasant . . .'

'Me!' said the young inspector, raising his hand like a schoolboy.

And Lucas said:

'Why don't we share the job? I can phone my wife to say that I won't be home for dinner. I'll have a sandwich in the bar opposite Montrouge Church. Later, Lapointe can come and relieve me. . . .'

'I'll be there about ten o'clock,' decided Lapointe.

'Later if you like. Why not divide the night in two and say midnight?'

'I'll be there earlier than that. If I'm not going to bed, I'd rather be doing something.'

'What orders, Chief?'

'None, boys. And, tomorrow, if they call me to account, I shall be hard put to it to explain this particular job. They've both been here, husband and wife. They've insisted, both of them, on telling me all about their little troubles. Logically speaking, nothing ought to happen. But it's precisely because . . .'

He did not finish what he had in mind, which was not clear enough to be put into words.

'Perhaps I did wrong in letting him know his wife had been here. I hesitated about it. Then I said to myself . . .'

He shrugged his shoulders, feeling sick of the whole business, and opened the cupboard where his hat and coat were hanging, growling:

'Anyway, we'll see what happens . . . Good night all the same, boys. . . .'

'Good night, Chief.'

And Lucas added:

'I'll be over there in an hour.'

Outside, the cold had become sharper and the snowflakes, hard and tiny, scarcely visible in the haloes of the street-lamps, pricked the skin, which they seemed to want to penetrate, settling on eyelashes, eyebrows and lips.

Maigret did not feel up to waiting for a bus and took a taxi, huddling in the back, well wrapped up in his heavy coat.

All the other cases he had investigated struck him as having been almost childishly simple compared with this one, and this annoyed him. Never had he felt so unsure of himself, to the extent of telephoning Pardon, going to see the chief and the Public Prosecutor, and, only a moment ago, angling for Lapointe's approval.

He had the impression of being all at sea. Then, while the taxi was going round the Place de la République, a thought came to him which comforted him a little.

If this case was unlike the others and if he did not know how to set about it, wasn't that because, this time, it was not a question of a crime which had already been committed, which only needed to be reconstructed, but of a crime which might be committed at any moment?

Just as it might quite well not be committed at all! How many potential crimes, crimes *in posse*, some of them meticulously prepared in the criminal's mind, are never perpetrated? How many people intend to do away with somebody, consider all the means of attaining this end and, at the last moment, lose their nerve?

Some cases which he had dealt with came back

to mind. Some of them would never have come to anything but for a favourable opportunity, or sometimes an accident. In certain cases, if, at a given moment, the victim had not pronounced some particular phrase, or assumed some particular attitude, nothing would have happened.

What he had to do, this time, was not to reconstruct the acts and gestures of a human being, but to forecast his behaviour, which was much more difficult.

None of the treatises on psychology, psychoanalysis or psychiatry were of any use to him.

He had known other couples of which one of the parties, for some reason, wanted the death of the other.

Precedents did not help him either. It is only with professionals that precedents can be turned to account, or else with certain maniacs. And then only with maniacs who have already killed one or more times and are repeating themselves.

He did not realize that the taxi had stopped at the kerb. The driver said to him:

'Here we are, Chief.'

The door of the flat opened as usual and Maigret rediscovered the light, the familiar smells, the furniture and the other objects which had been in their places for so many years.

He also rediscovered Madame Maigret's gaze which, as always, especially when she knew that he was worried, contained a mute inquiry.

'What do you say to going to the cinema?' he suggested.

'It's snowing!'

'You're afraid of catching cold?'

'No. I'd like to go to the cinema.'

She suspected that he did not want to stay in his armchair turning the same question over and over in his mind as he had done the evening before. An hour later, they were walking in the direction of the Place de la République and the Boulevard Bonne-Nouvelle, and Madame Maigret had hooked her hand on to her husband's arm.

Xavier Marton's sister-in-law, Jenny, had done the same thing when he had surprised her on the embankment. Maigret asked himself how long it had been, after their first meeting, before his wife had made that particular gesture.

A hundred yards from the cinema, where he did not even know what film they were showing, he put the question to her.

'Oh, I know that,' she said with a smile. 'I can remember it exactly. We'd known each other for three months. The week before, you'd kissed me, on the landing, and after that, you'd kissed me every night at the same place. One Tuesday, you took me to the Opéra-Comique, where they were doing *Carmen*, and I wore a blue taffeta dress. I could even tell you which perfume I'd used. On our way to the taxi, you didn't hold me, and you just gave me your hand to help me to get into the car.

'After the theatre, you asked me if I was hungry. We went towards the Grands Boulevards, where the Taverne Pousset was still in existence.

'I pretended to stumble because of my high

heels and I put my hand in your arm. My boldness impressed me so much that I started trembling, and you had the good sense to pretend you hadn't noticed anything.

'Coming out of the restaurant, I made the same gesture, and I've been doing the same ever since.'

In other words, Jenny, too, had got into the habit. It followed that she and her brother-in-law often went walking together in the streets.

Didn't that suggest that they made no secret of their love and that, contrary to what Marton had implied, Gisèle Marton knew all about it?

He went down to the box-office window, then made for the entrance, holding two pink tickets in his hand.

They were showing a thriller, with shots, fights, and a hard-boiled hero who jumped out of a window to land in an open car and who, in the middle of the town, knocking the driver out, took his place at the wheel, drove at a reckless speed, and got away from the police cars with their screaming sirens.

He smiled in spite of himself. As a matter of fact, he was enjoying himself. He managed to forget the Martons and the sister-in-law, the Harris whose name was Schwob, and the more or less complicated affairs of the two couples.

At the interval, he bought some sweets for his wife, for this was a tradition going back almost as far as Madame Maigret's gesture in taking his arm. Another tradition, while she was eating her sweets, was for him to smoke half a pipe in the entrance-hall, where he had a vague look at the posters advertising the films that were coming.

The snow was still falling when they came out and the flakes were thicker, so that you could see them trembling for a moment on the ground before dissolving.

People were walking with their heads down, to avoid getting flakes in their eyes. The next day, no doubt, the snow would be whitening the roofs and the parked cars.

'Taxi!'

He was afraid that his wife would catch cold. He thought she already looked thinner and even though he knew that it was on Pardon's orders, it worried him all the same. It seemed to him that she was going to become more fragile, that she might lose her optimism, her good humour.

As the car was drawing up in front of their home, in the Boulevard Richard-Lenoir, he murmured:

'Would you mind terribly if I didn't come in for another hour?'

In any other case, he would not have asked: he would just have told her that he had some work to do. This evening, it was a question of doing something which was not necessary, which had not even any justification, and he felt the need to apologize about it.

'Shall I wait up for you?'

'No. Go to bed. I might be delayed.'

He saw her cross the pavement looking for the key of the flat in her handbag.

'The church of Saint-Pierre de Montrouge,' he said to the driver.

The streets were almost empty, the roadway slippery, with serpentine tracks where cars had skidded.

'Not too fast . . .'

He was thinking:

'If anything is really going to happen . . .'

Why had he got the impression that it would be very soon? Xavier Marton had come to see him the day before. Not a week before, when the situation was the same, but only the day before. Didn't that indicate that the drama was coming to some sort of maturity?

Gisèle, too, had come to the Quai the day before.

And her husband had come again this very day.

He tried to remember what was said about this subject in the book on psychiatry he had dipped into. Perhaps, after all, he had been wrong not to take a greater interest in it? There were several pages about the development of crises, but he had skipped them.

Now, there was one thing which might bring the drama to a head, if there was a drama. Xavier Marton had agreed to undergo an examination the next day, at eleven o'clock in the morning, in the special infirmary at the *Dépôt*.

Would he mention it to his sister-in-law? To his wife? And would the latter pass on the news to her lover in the Rue Saint-Honoré?

Once the examination was over, and whatever

the result might be, it seemed certain that it would be too late for fresh developments.

The taxi stopped in front of the church. Maigret paid the fare. Opposite, a café-bar was still open, where there were only two or three customers. Maigret pushed open the door and ordered a toddy, not so much to warm himself up as because somebody had mentioned a toddy to him not long before. As he was making for the call-box the barman shouted to him:

'You want a *jeton*?

'I'm just going to have a look at the directory.'

For no particular reason, as it happened. Thinking about Monsieur Harris, he had wondered whether the Martons were on the telephone and he wanted to make sure.

They were not. Plenty of Mortons and Martins, but not a single Marton.

'What do I owe you?'

He turned into the Avenue de Châtillon, which was deserted and where there were only two or three windows still lighted. He could see neither Lucas nor Lapointe, and he was beginning to feel anxious when, about the middle of the Avenue, not far past the Rue Antoine-Chantin, he heard a voice near him say:

'Here, Chief . . .'

It was young Lapointe, huddled in a corner, a muffler covering half his face, his hands as deep as they would go in his coat pockets.

'I recognized your step as soon as you turned the corner of the avenue.'

'It's over there?' asked the chief-inspector,

pointing to an apartment-house in yellow brick where all the windows were in darkness.

'Yes. You see that dark gap, to the right of the door?'

It was a kind of blind alley, or passage, such as you often still see in Paris, even in the heart of the city. In a passage of this sort, off the Boulevard Saint-Martin, they had once found a murdered man, at five o'clock in the afternoon, a few yards from the crowds going by on the pavement.

'That leads into the courtyard?'

'Yes. They can go in and out without calling the concierge.'

'You've been to have a look?'

'I go every ten minutes. If you're going over there, mind how you walk. A huge ginger cat will come and quietly rub against your legs. The first time, it miaowed and I was afraid it would give the show away.'

'Have they gone to bed?'

'They hadn't a few minutes ago.'

'What are they doing?'

'I don't know. Somebody must still be up on the first floor, as there's a light on, but you can't see anything because of the blinds. I've waited in vain for a silhouette to appear; it looks as though the person or persons in the room aren't moving about or are staying at the back. There's a light on the ground floor as well. You don't realize it's there for some time, because the steel shutters only allow thin strips of light to shine through.'

Maigret crossed the road and Lapointe followed him. Both of them took care not to make any noise. The passage, which was vaulted over for three or four yards, was as cold and damp as a cellar. In the courtyard they found complete darkness and, as they stood still, a cat came sure enough and rubbed against, not the chief-inspector, but Lapointe, whom it already seemed to have adopted.

'They've gone to bed,' whispered the inspector. 'The lighted window was just in front of you.'

He tip-toed up to the shutters on the ground floor, bent down, then came back to the chief-inspector. Just as the two men were about to turn away, a light went on, not in the cottage, but on the second floor of the block of flats.

They both stood stock-still in the shadows, afraid that they had been heard by one of the tenants, and expecting to see a face pressed against the window-pane.

Nothing of the kind happened. A shadow passed behind the curtain. They heard a cistern flush.

'Somebody piddling,' sighed Lapointe in relief.

A moment later, they were back on the opposite pavement. Curiously enough, they were almost disappointed, the two of them. It was Lapointe who murmured:

'They've gone to bed.'

Didn't that mean that nothing was going to happen, that the chief-inspector had been worrying needlessly?

'I wonder . . .' began Maigret.

Two policemen on bicycles appeared, heading straight towards them. They had spotted them from a distance and, from the kerb, one of the two challenged them in a loud voice:

'What are you two up to?'

Maigret stepped forward. The beam of an electric torch picked out his face. The policeman frowned.

'You aren't . . . ? Oh! I beg your pardon, sir . . . I didn't recognize you at first . . .'

He added, after a glance at the house opposite:

'Do you want us to lend a hand?'

'Not at the moment.'

'Anyway, we come by every hour.'

The two men in their capes moved off, sprinkled with snow, and Maigret rejoined Lapointe, who had not stirred.

'What was I saying?'

'That you were wondering . . .'

'Ah, yes . . . I was wondering whether husband and wife still slept in the same bed. . . .'

'I don't know. From what Janvier told me this afternoon, there's a divan on the ground floor, though that doesn't necessarily mean somebody sleeps on it. Logically speaking, if anybody uses it, it ought to be the sister-in-law, don't you think?'

'Good night, old chap. Perhaps you can . . .'

He wondered if he should send Lapointe home to bed. What was the use of mounting guard in front of a house where nothing was happening?

'If it's on my account you're hesitating . . .'

In point of fact, Lapointe would be annoyed not to see the job through to the end.

'Stay if you like. Good night. You don't want to go and have a drink?'

'I must admit I went and had one a few minutes before you arrived. From the bar on the corner, I could see the whole street.'

When Maigret arrived at Saint-Pierre de Montrouge, the gates of the Metro were shut and there was not a single taxi in sight. He hesitated between heading towards the Lion de Belfort and going down the Avenue du Maine in the direction of the Gare Montparnasse. He decided on the Avenue du Maine because of the station, and in fact he soon hailed a taxi coming away from the station empty.

'Boulevard Richard-Lenoir.'

He had not got the key of the flat, but he knew he would find it under the door-mat. For all that he was head of the Criminal Squad, he had never thought of telling his wife that this hiding-place was, to say the least, illusory.

She was asleep and he started undressing in the half-light, only leaving the corridor lamp on. A few moments later, a voice from the bed asked:

'Is it late?'

'I don't know. Half past one perhaps . . .'

'You haven't caught cold?'

'No.'

'You don't want me to make you a hot drink?'

'No, thanks, I had a toddy a little while ago.'

'And you went out again afterwards?'

These were ordinary little phrases which he had heard hundreds of times, but they struck him tonight because he wondered whether Gisèle Marton had ever pronounced them.

Wasn't it precisely for want of hearing them that her husband . . . ?

'You can put the light on.'

He just switched on the bedside lamp, on his side of the bed, and went and turned out the light in the corridor.

'You're sure you've shut the hall door?'

He would not have been surprised to hear his wife get up, in a few minutes, to go and make certain.

That too formed part of a whole, a whole which Xavier Marton had no doubt looked for, which he had not found, which . . .

He slipped between the warm sheets, turned out the light, and in the dark, without fumbling, found his wife's lips.

He thought he would find it difficult to get off to sleep and yet, a few moments later, he was asleep. It is true that, if the light had been turned on suddenly, it would have been seen that he was wearing a frown, an expression of concentration, as if he were still in pursuit of a truth which was slipping away.

As a rule, Madame Maigret got up quietly at half past six and went to the kitchen without his noticing. He only began to become aware of the new day when the smell of coffee reached him.

It was the time when other windows lit up on

the Boulevard Richard-Lenoir and in every part of Paris, the time when the footsteps of early risers could be heard on the pavements.

That day he was not roused from sleep by the familiar smell of coffee, nor by his wife's noiseless tread. It was the telephone bell, suddenly ringing, that snatched him out of the world of darkness and, when he opened his eyes, Madame Maigret, already sitting up in bed, was shaking him by the shoulder.

'What time is it?' he stammered.

She groped about for the button on the bedside lamp, then the light shone on the alarmclock and the hands were pointing to ten to six.

'Hullo!' said Maigret in a thick voice. 'Is that you, Lapointe?'

'Chief-Inspector Maigret?'

He could not recognize the voice, and frowned.

'Who's that speaking?'

'This is the emergency service. Inspector Joffre.'

It sometimes happened, in certain specific cases, that he left instructions with the emergency service to get in touch with him direct if something in particular occurred. He had not done anything of the sort the day before. His ideas were not connecting yet. However, he was only slightly surprised.

'What is it, Joffre? Is it Lapointe?'

'What about Lapointe?'

'Is it Lapointe who's asked you to ring me up?'

'I haven't had any news from Lapointe. Just a phone call, a moment ago, asking us to pass a message on to you.'

'What message?'

'To go straight away to the Avenue de Châtillon . . . Hang on! I made a note of the number . . .'

'I know it. Who was it speaking?'

'I don't know. They didn't give a name.'

'A man? A woman?'

'A woman. She says you know all about it and that you'll know what it means. It seems that she looked for your number in the directory but that . . .'

Maigret was not listed in the directory.

'There's nothing I can do for you?'

The chief-inspector hesitated. He nearly asked Joffre to telephone on his behalf to the police station in the XIVth *arrondissement* to ask them to send someone to the Avenue de Châtillon. Then, on reflection, he decided not to. Sitting on the edge of his bed, he felt around with his feet for his slippers. As for his wife, she was already in the kitchen and he heard the pop of the gas on which she was putting some water to heat.

'Nothing, thanks . . .'

What surprised him was that it was not Lapointe who had rung him up, although he was on the spot.

Which woman had it been? Gisèle Marton? The sister-in-law?

If it was one of those two, she could not have left the apartment-house, for Lapointe would have seen her and telephoned Maigret himself.

Now, the Martons were not on the telephone.

He called his wife.

'While I'm getting dressed, will you look in the telephone directory, the one with the classification by streets, and see who's on the telephone at No. 17, Avenue de Châtillon?'

He hesitated about shaving, and decided not to, despite his reluctance to go out like that, in order to save time.

'No. 17 . . . Here we are . . . Apartment-house . . .'

'Good. That means there's a telephone in the lodge.'

'I can see a Madame Boussard too, a midwife. That's all. There'll be some coffee for you in two minutes.'

He ought to have told Joffre to send him one of the cars from the Quai des Orfèvres, but now it would take longer than calling a taxi.

Madame Maigret said she would see to this. Five minutes later, after scalding his mouth swallowing coffee that was too hot, the chief-inspector was going downstairs.

'Will you ring me up?' asked his wife, leaning over the banisters.

This was something she rarely asked him. She must have sensed that he was more worried than usual.

He promised:

'I'll try.'

The taxi arrived. He plunged into it, scarcely noticing that it was not snowing any more, that there were no white patches in the street or on

140

the roofs, but that an icy rain was blackening the roadway.

'Avenue de Châtillon.'

He gave a sniff, for the taxi still smelt of scent. No doubt it had just taken home a couple who had spent the night dancing in a fashionable restaurant. A little later, he bent down and picked up a little ball of pink cotton-wool such as grown-ups throw at one another, after midnight, while they are drinking champagne.

7

MAIGRET had asked to be set down at the corner of the Avenue de Châtillon and, as in his own district, the pavements were deserted in the rain; as in the Boulevard Richard-Lenoir too, there were a few lighted windows, three or four in each block; in the time it took him to walk a hundred yards, he saw two light up, and heard, on a ground floor that was still dark, an alarm-clock ringing.

He looked to see if Lapointe was in his corner, could not find him, and growled a few syllables under his breath, disgruntled, anxious, only half-awake.

In the passage-way into the yellow-brick apartment-house, he finally saw a very short woman, with hips as broad as her shoulders, who was obviously the concierge, a Metro employee holding in his hand the tin box containing his dinner, and another woman, an old one this time, her white hair in curling-pins, dressed in a sky-blue woollen dressing-gown and a shawl of a violent purple colour.

All three looked at him in silence and it was only later that he discovered what had happened, and found out why Lapointe was not outside on the pavement. For some moments, at the very least, he had felt an emptiness in his chest, for he had thought that as the result of circumstances which he did not try to imagine, his inspector was perhaps the victim.

As usual, it was simpler than that. When Gisèle Marton had come to telephone from the lodge, the concierge was up and busy making coffee, but she had not yet put out the dustbins. She had heard a call being made to the emergency service, then the message from her tenant, who had left the lodge without giving her the least information.

The concierge had gone and opened one half of the door, as she did every morning, before dragging the dustbins out on to the pavement. Just at that moment Lapointe had been crossing the road, with the intention of having a look inside the courtyard as he had done several times during the night. Because of the telephone call which she had just heard, the woman had looked at him suspiciously.

'What do you want?'

'I suppose nothing out of the ordinary has happened in the house?'

He showed her his badge.

'You're from the police, are you? Well now, there's somebody at the back of the courtyard who's just sent for the police. What's happening, with all these goings-on?'

That was how Lapointe had come to cross the courtyard, without any attempt at concealment, this time, and knock at the door, under which he could see a strip of light. The three windows on the first floor were lighted too.

Maigret, for his part, had no need to knock. His footsteps had been heard and it was Lapointe who, from the inside, opened the door to him, a Lapointe pale from fatigue, and also from what he had just found. He did not say a word, the sight which met his chief's eyes speaking for itself.

The divan in the studio-cum-sitting-room did in fact turn into a bed at night and it was Xavier Marton who used it. The sheets were in disorder, the pillow askew, and on the floor, on the beige-coloured jute carpet, half-way between the bed and the spiral staircase leading to the first floor, was the body of the electric-train enthusiast, dressed in pyjamas, and lying face down.

The red stripes of the pyjamas gave added emphasis to the contortion of the body. One had the impression that he had collapsed while crawling on all fours and he was all twisted, his right arm stretched out in front, his hands clenched, as if, in a final effort, he had tried to reach the revolver which was also lying on the floor, about eight inches away from his fingers.

Maigret did not ask whether he was dead. That was obvious. Three people were looking at him in silence, for the two women were there, almost as motionless as the corpse, in their nightwear too, with dressing-gowns over their nightdresses, and their bare feet in slippers. Jenny's hair, which was darker than her sister's, was partly falling over her face and hiding one of her eyes.

Automatically, without thinking of what he was saying, Maigret murmured to Lapointe:

'You haven't touched anything?'

Lapointe shook his head. There were shadows under his eyes, and his beard, like the dead man's and Maigret's, had grown during the night.

'Notify the local police station. Telephone the Criminal Records Office and ask them to send us photographers and experts straight away. Ring up Dr. Paul as well. . . .'

'And the Parquet?'

'There'll be time for that later.'

In that part of the *Palais de Justice* life did not begin as early as at the Quai des Orfèvres and Maigret did not want to have those gentlemen getting in his way sooner than he could help.

He looked at the two women. Neither of them had thought of sitting down. With her back to the wall, by the table for the electric train, the sister-in-law, holding a handkerchief rolled into a ball in one hand, kept dabbing her red eyes, and sniffing as if she had a cold in the head. She had big dark eyes, which were soft and timorous, rather like the eyes of forest animals, of squirrels for example, and she gave off a warm smell of bed.

Colder or more composed, Gisèle Marton was watching the chief-inspector and from time to time her hands contracted in an involuntary movement.

Lapointe had gone out and crossed the courtyard. He would be busy telephoning from the concierge's lodge. The two women were doubtless expecting Maigret to question them. Perhaps for a moment he had thought of doing so, but, in the end, he just said in a low voice:

'Go and get dressed.'

This baffled them, Jenny even more than Gisèle. She opened her mouth to speak, said nothing, and decided, after a hard look of bitter hatred at her sister, to go upstairs first; while she was going up, the chief-inspector could see her bare white thighs.

'You too . . .'

In a rather hoarse voice, Gisèle said:

'I know.'

She seemed to be waiting until her sister had shut herself in her room before going up herself.

Maigret only remained alone with Marton's body for a few moments, and he scarcely had time to make an inventory of the room with his eyes. The room was none the less photographed in his mind, down to its smallest details, and he knew that he would be able to find them again in his memory when he needed them.

He heard a car stopping, brakes squealing, a door slamming shut. Then there were footsteps in the courtyard and, just as Lapointe had done for him, he opened the door.

He knew Boisset, the inspector of the XIVth *arrondissement*, who was accompanied by a policeman in uniform and a tubby little man carrying a doctor's bag.

'Come in, all three of you . . . I think, Doctor, that all you've got to do is to certify the death . . . Dr. Paul will be here before long . . .'

Boisset looked inquiringly at him.

'A case I've been dealing with for the last two days,' murmured Maigret. 'I'll explain later . . . At the moment, there's nothing to be done . . .'

They heard footsteps overhead, the noise of a tap, a cistern flushing.

As Boisset raised his eyes in surprise towards the ceiling, Maigret added:

'The wife and the sister-in-law . . .'

He felt as weary as if it had been he, and not Lapointe, who had spent the night outside, in the cold and the rain. The inspector was soon back. The doctor, after kneeling for a moment, stood up again. He had shone an electric torch into the dead man's staring eyes; then he had put his face close to the man's lips and sniffed.

'At first sight, it looks like a case of poisoning.'

'It *is* a case of poisoning.'

Lapointe motioned to Maigret that he had completed his mission. Voices could be heard whispering in the courtyard. Several people had come up to the shutters, which were still closed.

Maigret said to the policeman in uniform:

'You might go out and stop them gathering together.'

The doctor asked:

'Do you need me any more?'

'No. You'll be given the identification details later for the death certificate.'

'Good-bye, gentlemen! Boisset knows where to find me.'

Gisèle Marton came down first and Maigret noticed straight away that she was wearing her costume and carrying her fur coat on her arm. She was also holding a handbag, which suggested that she expected to be taken away. She had seized the opportunity to make up, in a discreet way. The expression on her face was serious and thoughtful, with a few traces of shock still apparent.

When Jenny in her turn appeared, she was wearing a black dress. Noticing her sister's outfit, she asked, after wetting her lips:

'Shall I fetch my coat?'

Maigret blinked his eyes. The one who was watching him most closely was Lapointe, who had rarely been so impressed by his chief's behaviour . . . He sensed that this was not an ordinary investigation, and that the chief-inspector did not intend to use ordinary methods, but he had not the faintest idea what he meant to do.

Everyone's nerves were so on edge that it was a relief to see Boisset light a cigarette. He offered his packet to Lapointe, who refused, then, noticing Gisèle who stood waiting as if she were on a station platform, he said:

'Do you smoke?'

She took one. He held the flame of his lighter up to her cigarette, and she began breathing in nervously.

'Have you got a police car at the door?' Maigret asked the local inspector.

'I kept it in case.'

'Can I use it?'

He was still looking all round as if to make sure that he was not forgetting a single detail. He was about to give the two women the signal to go when he changed his mind.

'One moment . . .'

And he went upstairs himself, alone, to the first floor, where the lights had been left on. There were only two bedrooms, a bathroom and a lumber-room where suitcases, old trunks and a dressmaker's dummy were piled together, with two old oil-lamps and some dusty books lying on the floor.

He went into the first bedroom, the bigger of the two. It contained a small double bed and the smell told him that he was in Madame Marton's room. The wardrobe confirmed him in this opinion, for in it he found clothes of the sort he knew she wore, simple, elegant, even rich. On a shelf a little way above the floor, a dozen pairs of shoes were arranged in a row.

The bed was unmade, like the one downstairs. The nightdress and the salmon-pink dressing-gown had been carelessly thrown on to it. On the dressing-table, pots of cream, bottles, a silver manicure-set, and some pins in a Chinese bowl.

In another wardrobe, some men's clothes, just two suits, a sports jacket, two pairs of shoes, and some sandals. There was obviously no wardrobe downstairs and Marton had gone on leaving his things in the double bedroom.

He opened the chest of drawers, pushed a door, and found himself in the bathroom. On the glass shelf, he saw three toothmugs, with a toothbrush in each one, which suggested that each person came here in turn. Lipstick on some crumpled towels, one of which had been thrown on the floor. And, on the porcelain bowl of the lavatory, and on the tiled floor round it, some little dried-up stains, as if someone, in the course of the night, had been sick.

The other bedroom did not connect with the bathroom. You had to go through the corridor. It was smaller, with a blue floral wallpaper, and the bed was a single bed.

There was greater disorder here than in the first bedroom. The wardrobe door had been left open. There was a tweed coat bearing the label of a New York firm. Far fewer shoes, only four pairs in fact, two of which also came from America. Finally, on the table covered with an embroidered cloth which served as a dressing-table, a jumble of incongruous objects: a pencil with the lead broken, a fountain-pen, some small change, combs, hairpins, and a brush which had lost some of its bristles.

Maigret went on registering. When he went downstairs again, he looked as slow-witted as before, with eyes which scarcely moved.

He discovered that the kitchen was on the ground floor, behind a partition which had been built in one corner of what had been the carpenter's workshop. He pushed the door open, while Gisèle Marton continued to follow him with her eyes. The kitchen was minute. It comprised a gas-cooker, a white cupboard, a sink, and a table covered with oilcloth.

There was no crockery lying around. The porcelain of the sink was dry.

He went back to the others, who were still as motionless as if they were in a waxworks.

'You'll receive the gentlemen of the Parquet,' he said to Lapointe. 'Tender my apologies to Dr. Paul for not waiting for him. Ask him to telephone me as soon as he's done the necessary. I'll send you somebody, I don't know yet whom . . .'

He turned to the two women.

'If you will follow me . . .'

Of the two, the sister-in-law was the more frightened and it seemed as if she were reluctant to leave the house. Gisèle, on the other hand, had opened the door and, standing very upright, was waiting in the rain.

The policeman had shepherded the inquisitive spectators out of the courtyard, but he could not prevent them forming a circle opposite the passage, on the pavement. The old woman was still there, with her purple shawl over her head in lieu of an umbrella. The Metro employee must have had to go off, regretfully, to his work.

They looked at them as the public always looks at these comings and goings which strike it as at once mysterious and dramatic. The policeman pushed back the crowd to clear a way to the car and the chief-inspector let the two women go in front of him.

A voice said:

'He's arresting them . . .'

He shut the door after them, and went round the car to take his place beside the uniformed driver.

'Headquarters.'

One could feel, albeit vaguely, the beginning of a new day. The rain was turning grey, the sky a dirty colour. They drove past some buses, and half-awake people were diving down the Metro staircases.

When they got to the embankments, the street-lamps had lost nearly all their brilliance and the towers of Notre-Dame were standing out against the sky.

The car entered the courtyard. During the

journey, the two women had not said a word, but one of them, Jenny, had sniffed several times. Once, she had given her nose a long blow. When she got out of the car, her nose was red, like Marton's on his first visit.

'This way, ladies.'

He went in front of them up the big staircase which was in process of being swept, pushed open the glass door, and looked for Joseph whom he could not see. He ended up by showing them into his office, where he turned on the lights, and glanced inside the inspectors' office, where there were only three men, three who knew nothing about the case.

He picked Janin out at random.

'Will you stay for a minute in my office with these ladies?'

And, turning towards them:

'Sit down, please. I suppose you haven't had any coffee?'

Jenny did not reply. Madame Marton shook her head.

Ostentatiously, Maigret went to the door, locked it from the inside, and put the key in his pocket.

'You'd be well advised to sit down,' he repeated, 'because you'll be here for some time.'

He went into the other office.

'Baron! Telephone the Brasserie Dauphine, will you. Tell them to send up a big pot of coffee. Black coffee . . . Three cups and some *croissants* . . .'

After which, he dropped into a chair near the window, picked up another telephone, and asked to be put through to the Public Prosecutor. The latter could only just have got up and was doubtless busy dressing or having his breakfast. However, it was not a servant who answered, but he himself.

'Maigret here, sir. Marton is dead . . . The man I spoke to you about yesterday morning . . . No, I'm at the Quai des Orfèvres . . . I've left an inspector at the Avenue de Châtillon—Lapointe . . . Dr. Paul has been notified . . . Criminal Records too, yes . . . I don't know . . . I've got the two women in my office . . .'

He spoke in a low voice, although the communicating door between the two rooms was shut.

'I don't think I can go over there this morning . . . I'm going to send another inspector to relieve Lapointe . . .'

He wore a rather guilty expression. When the conversation was over, he looked at his watch, and decided to wait for Janvier, who would not be long now and who was familiar with the case, to send him to the scene of the crime.

After passing his hand over his cheeks, he asked the third inspector, Bonfils, who was busy writing his report on the night's minor incidents:

'Will you go to my cupboard and get my razor, shaving-brush and towel?'

He preferred not to do this himself in front of the two women. With his shaving-kit in his hand, he went down the corridor and into the cloak-room, where he took his jacket off and shaved. He took his time over it, as if to put off the moment when he would have to do what remained to be done. After washing his face in cold water, he rejoined his colleagues and, in addition, the waiter from the Brasserie Dauphine, who did not know where to put his tray.

'In my office . . . This way . . .'

He picked up the telephone again and this time it was to his wife that he spoke.

'I'm going to have a busy morning. I don't know yet whether I'll be able to come home for lunch.'

Because of his tired voice, she anxiously asked:

'There's nothing wrong, is there?'

What could he say in reply?

'Don't worry. I'm going to have my breakfast.'

Finally he gave instructions to Bonfils:

'When Janvier arrives, tell him to come and see me.'

He went into his office, which the waiter was just leaving, and released Janin. Then, still as if he were acting in slow motion, or as if he were in a dream, he poured coffee into the three cups.

'Sugar?' he asked, addressing Gisèle Marton first.

'Two lumps.'

He handed her her cup, and the plate of *croissants*, but she gave a sign that she did not want anything to eat.

'Sugar?'

The sister-in-law shook her head. She did not eat anything either, and he was the only one to nibble, without any appetite, at a *croissant* that was still warm.

The day had dawned, but it was not bright enough yet to turn out the lights. Twice, Jenny had opened her mouth to ask a question and both times a look from the chief-inspector had robbed her of any desire to speak.

The moment had come. Maigret, who had poured himself out a second cup of coffee, was slowly filling a pipe chosen from among the pipes scattered about on his desk.

Standing up, he looked at each of the women in turn.

'I think I'll begin with you,' he murmured, stopping at Madame Marton.

Jenny gave a slight start and, once again, tried to say something.

'As for you, I'd like you to wait in another room with one of my inspectors.'

He called Janin back.

'You'll take this lady into the green office and you'll stay with her until I call you.'

This was not the first time this had happened. They were used to it.

'Right, Chief.'

'Janvier still isn't there?'

'I think I heard his voice in the corridor.'

'Tell him to come here straight away.'

Janin went off with the sister-in-law. A moment later, Janvier came in, and stopped short in surprise at the sight of Madame Marton sitting in a chair, a cup of coffee in her hand.

'Marton is dead,' said Maigret. 'Lapointe is on the spot. He's spent the night outside and you'd do well to go and relieve him.'

'No instructions, Chief?'

'Lapointe will pass them on to you. If you take a car, you'll still get there before the Parquet.'

'You won't be coming?'

'I don't think so.'

Both doors were finally shut and there was nobody left in the office but Maigret and Madame Marton. It seemed as if she had been waiting for this particular moment and, while he remained silent in front of her, drawing on his pipe, she slowly came back to life, emerging little by little from her torpor, or rather from her rigidity.

It was strange to see her face becoming human once more, her complexion colouring slightly, her eyes expressing something other than expectation.

'You think I've poisoned him, don't you?'

He took his time. It was not the first time that he had refrained, as he had done that morning, from asking questions as soon as a crime was discovered. It is often preferable not to have people speaking too soon, whether they are suspects or witnesses, for if, right at the beginning, they have made a statement, they often stick to it later for fear of being accused of lying.

He had deliberately given them, both of them,

time to think, time to decide on their attitude and the statements they would make.

'I don't think anything,' he murmured at last. 'You will have noticed that I haven't called in the stenographer. I shan't take any notes of what you say to me. Just tell me what happened.'

He knew that his composure, the simple way in which he spoke to her, puzzled her.

'Begin, for example, with yesterday evening.'

'What do you want to know?'

'Everything.'

It was embarrassing. She wondered where to begin her story and in spite of everything he gave her a little help.

'You came home . . .'

'As I do every night of course.'

'At what time?'

'Eight o'clock. After closing the shop, I had an *apéritif* in a bar in the Rue Castiglione.'

'With Monsieur Harris?'

'Yes.'

'And then?'

'My husband had come home before me. My sister was in too. We sat down at table.'

'It was your sister who'd cooked the dinner?'

'As usual.'

'You eat downstairs, in the living-room which serves your husband as a workshop and a bed-room at the same time?'

'Several months ago, he decided to sleep there.'

'How many months ago?'

She did some mental arithmetic. Her lips moved.

'Eight months,' she said in the end.

'What did you eat?'

'First of all, soup . . . The same as the day before . . . Jenny always makes enough soup for two days. . . . Then ham and salad, cheese and pears. . . .'

'Coffee?'

'We never drink coffee in the evening.'

'You didn't notice anything unusual?'

She hesitated, looking him straight in the eye.

'That depends on what you call unusual. I don't quite know what to tell you, because I suspect that there are certain things you know better than I do. The proof of that is that there was an inspector at the door. Before sitting down to dinner, I went upstairs to take my coat off and get into slippers. That was how I found out that my sister had been out and that she'd only just got back.'

'How did you find out?'

'Because I opened the door of her room and saw some shoes of hers that were still wet. Her coat was damp too.'

'Why did you go into her room?'

'Just to make sure that she'd been out.'

'Why?'

Still not averting her eyes, she replied:

'So as to know.'

'Jenny cleared the table?'

'Yes.'

'It's always she who clears away?'

'She insists on paying her share by doing the housework.'

'She does the washing-up too?'

'Sometimes my husband gives her a hand.'

'Not you?'

'No.'

'Go on.'

'She made some herbal tea, as she did every evening. It was she who got us into the habit of drinking herbal tea, at night.'

'Lime-blossom? Camomile?'

'No. Chinese anise. My sister has a sluggish liver. Since she came back from the States, she's had a cup of Chinese anise every night, and my husband wanted to try it, and then I copied him. You know how it is . . .'

'She brought in the cups on a tray?'

'Yes.'

'With the teapot?'

'No. She filled the cups in the kitchen and then came and put the tray on the table.'

'What was your husband doing just then?'

'He was trying to get a station on the radio.'

'So that, if I remember the room correctly, he had his back to you?'

'Yes.'

'What were you doing?'

'I'd just opened a magazine.'

'Near the table?'

'Yes.'

'And your sister?'

'She went back to the kitchen to start the washing-up. I know what you're getting at, but I'll tell you the truth all the same. I didn't put anything in the cups, either in my husband's or in the others. I just took a precaution which I've been taking for some time whenever possible.'

'What's that?'

'Unobtrusively turning the tray so that the cup which is meant for me becomes my husband's or my sister's.'

'And, last night, your cup became . . . ?'

'My husband's.'

'He drank it?'

'Yes. He picked it up and then put it on the radio. . . .'

'You didn't at any moment leave the room? There couldn't have been another substitution?'

'I've been thinking about that for nearly two hours.'

'And what conclusion have you reached?'

'Before my sister brought the tray in, my husband went to the kitchen. Jenny will probably deny it, but it's the truth.'

'What did he go there for?'

'Ostensibly to see whether his spectacles were there. He wears spectacles for reading. He needs them too to see the control panel of the radio. From the studio, you can hear everything that is said in the kitchen. He didn't speak to my sister, came back almost immediately, and found his spectacles by the electric train.'

'It was because of this visit to the kitchen that you changed the cups round?'

'Possibly. Not necessarily. As I've just told you, I often did it.'

'Because you were afraid of his poisoning you?'

She looked at him without answering.

'What happened next?'

'Nothing different from any other evening. My sister came and drank her tea and went back to the kitchen. Xavier listened to a programme on the radio while he repaired a little electric motor he meant to use for something or other.'

'And you went on reading?'

'For an hour or two. It was about ten o'clock when I went upstairs.'

'You went first?'

'Yes.'

'What was your sister doing then?'

'She was making my husband's bed.'

'You were in the habit of leaving them alone together?'

'Why not? What difference could it make?'

'You think they took the opportunity to kiss each other?'

'If they did, it's all the same to me.'

'Have you any reason to believe that your husband was your sister's lover?'

'I don't know if they were lovers. I doubt it. He behaved like a boy of seventeen with her.'

'Why did you say "I doubt it" just now?'

She did not reply immediately. Maigret's gaze was insistent. Finally she answered his question with another question.

'Why do you think we haven't any children?'

'Because you didn't want any.'

'That's what he told you, isn't it? And it's

probably what he told his colleagues. A man doesn't like to admit that he's impotent.'

'That was the case, was it?'

She nodded, not without a certain weariness.

'Look here, Chief-Inspector, there are still a lot of things you don't know. Xavier gave you his version of our life. When I came to see you, I didn't bother to go into details. Things happened last night which I don't understand and I know that, when I tell you about them, you won't believe me.'

He did not hurry her. He wanted, on the contrary, to give her plenty of time to speak, and even to weigh her words.

'I heard the doctor, this morning, saying that Xavier had been poisoned. That may be true. But so had I.'

He could not help giving a start, and looking at her more closely.

'You had been poisoned?'

He remembered something which made him feel inclined to believe her: the stains, already dry, on the porcelain of the lavatory and on the tiling.

'I woke up about the middle of the night with horrible burning pains in the stomach. When I got up, I was surprised to feel light-headed and weak in the legs. I made a dash for the bathroom, and I stuck two fingers into my mouth to make myself sick. I'm sorry if this isn't very pleasant. It was like fire, with an after-taste that I would recognize among a thousand others.'

'Did you call your sister, or your husband?'

'No. They may have heard me, because I pulled the chain several times. Twice, I washed my stomach out, and both times I brought up a liquid which left the same after-taste.'

'You didn't think of calling a doctor?'

'What for? Seeing that I'd tackled it in time. . . .'

'You went back to bed?'

'Yes.'

'You weren't tempted to go downstairs?'

'I just listened. I heard Xavier tossing about in his bed as if he were sleeping badly.'

'You realize that it was his cup you drank?'

'I suppose so.'

'You still maintain that you changed the cups round on the tray?'

'Yes.'

'And, afterwards, you didn't let the tray out of your sight? Your husband, or your sister, couldn't have effected another substitution?'

'My sister was in the kitchen.'

'So your husband must have taken the cup that was meant for you?'

'It looks like it.'

'Which amounts to saying that it was your sister who tried to poison your husband?'

'I don't know.'

'Or else, seeing that your husband was poisoned as well, that she tried to poison both of you?'

She said again:

'I don't know.'

They looked at each other for a long time. In the end, it was Maigret who broke contact and went and planted himself in front of the window where, looking at the Seine flowing by in the rain, he filled another pipe.

8

PRESSING his forehead against the cold window-pane, as he used to do when he was a child and kept it there until the skin turned white and he felt pins and needles in his head, Maigret, without realizing it, followed the movements of two workmen who, on the other side of the Seine, were working on some scaffolding.

When he turned round, his face wore an expression of resignation and, making for his desk and sitting down at it again, he said, taking care not to look at Gisèle Marton:

'Have you anything else to tell me?'

She did not hesitate for long and, when she spoke, he could not help looking up, for in calm, measured tones, without either defiance or despondency, she said:

'I saw Xavier die.'

Did she know what sort of impression she

made on the chief-inspector? Did she realize that she inspired in him an involuntary, almost professional admiration? He could not remember seeing, in this office where so many people had appeared in turn, a being possessed of such lucidity and sang-froid. He could not remember either anybody so *detached*.

It was impossible to detect in her the slightest human vibration. There was not a single flaw in her make-up.

With his elbows on his blotting-pad, he sighed:

'Fire away.'

'I had gone back to bed and I was finding it hard to get to sleep again. I was trying to understand, without any success, what had happened. I no longer had any clear idea of the passage of time. You know how it is. You get the impression of following a continuous line of thought, but, in reality, there are gaps. I must have dozed off several times. Once or twice, I seemed to hear a noise downstairs, the noise my husband made turning over suddenly in his bed. At least that's what I thought.

'Once, I'm sure, I caught the sound of a groan and I said to myself that he was having nightmares. It wasn't the first time he'd talked and struggled in his sleep. He'd told me that, as a boy, he used to walk in his sleep, and he did that several times with me.'

She continued to choose her words carefully, without any more emotion than if she had been telling a story.

'At one point, I heard a louder noise, as if

something heavy had fallen on the floor. I hesitated about getting up, because I felt frightened. Straining my ears, I thought I could make out a rattling groan. I got up then, slipped my dressing-gown on, and quietly made for the stairs.'

'You didn't see your sister?'

'No.'

'And you didn't hear any sound from her bedroom? There wasn't a light under her door?'

'No. To see into the downstairs room, I had to go down several steps and I hesitated, conscious of some danger. I went down, all the same, reluctantly. I bent forward.'

'How many steps did you go down?'

'Six or seven. I didn't count them. There was a light in the studio, just the bedside lamp. Xavier was lying on the floor, roughly half-way between his bed and the spiral staircase. It looked as if he had been crawling along, as if he were still crawling along. He had raised himself on one elbow, the left elbow, and his right arm was stretched out in front to try to grasp the revolver lying about a foot away from his hand.'

'Did he see you?'

'Yes. Raising his head, he gave me a look of bitter hatred, his face all distorted, and froth or saliva on his lips. I realized that, as he was walking towards the stairs, already weakened, holding his gun in his hand, in order to kill me, his strength had failed him, he had fallen down and the revolver had rolled out of his reach.'

His eyes half-shut, Maigret recalled the studio, the staircase going up towards the ceiling, and Marton's body as it had been found.

'You continued to go downstairs?'

'No. I stayed there, incapable of taking my eyes off him. I couldn't be sure exactly how much energy he had left. I was hypnotized.'

'How long did he take to die?'

'I don't know. He kept trying both to reach the gun and to speak, to shout insults or threats at me. At the same time, he was afraid that I should come down, get hold of the revolver before him and shoot. That was doubtless partly why I didn't go down. I don't know for certain. I wasn't thinking. He was breathing hard. Some spasms shook him. I thought that he was going to be sick too. Then he gave a howl, his body shook several times, his hands contracted and finally, all of a sudden, he was still.'

Without averting her eyes, she added:

'I realized that it was all over.'

'It was then that you went down to make sure that he was dead?'

'No. I knew that he was. I don't know why I felt so certain. I went back to my room and sat on the edge of my bed. I felt cold. I put the blanket round my shoulders.'

'Your sister still hadn't left her room?'

'No.'

'Yet you said just now that he gave a howl.'

'That is correct. She must have heard it. She couldn't help hearing it, but she stayed in bed.'

'You didn't think of calling a doctor? Or of telephoning the police?'

'If there had been a telephone in the house, I might have done so. I can't be sure.'

'What time was it?'

'I don't know. I didn't think of looking at the alarm-clock. I was still trying to understand.'

'If you'd been on the telephone, wouldn't you have rung up your friend Harris?'

'Certainly not. He's married.'

'So you don't know, even approximately, how long it was from the time you saw your husband die to the time, about six o'clock in the morning, when you went to telephone from the concierge's lodge? Was it an hour? Two hours? Three hours?'

'Over an hour, I could swear to that. Less than three.'

'You expected to be arrested?'

'I hadn't any illusions.'

'And you wondered what you'd say to the questions you were going to be asked?'

'Possibly. Without realizing. I thought a great deal. Then I heard the familiar sound of dustbins being dragged across a nearby courtyard and I went downstairs.'

'Still without meeting your sister?'

'Yes. On the way, I touched my husband's hand. It was already cold. I looked for your telephone number in the directory and, as I couldn't find it, I rang the emergency service and asked them to notify you.'

'After which you went back to the house?'

'From the courtyard, I saw a light in my sister's room. When I opened the door, Jenny was coming downstairs.'

'She'd already seen the body?'

'Yes.'

'She didn't say anything?'

'She might have said something if there hadn't been a knock at the door almost immediately. It was your inspector.'

She added after a pause:

'If there's a little coffee left . . .'

'It's cold.'

'That doesn't matter.'

He gave her some, and poured out a cup for himself too.

Beyond the door, beyond the window, life was going on, everyday life, life as men had organized it to reassure themselves.

Here, between these four walls, there was another world, which could be felt palpitating behind every word, every phrase, a dark and fearful world, in which the young woman none the less seemed to move about easily.

'Did you love Marton?' asked Maigret in a low voice, almost despite himself.

'No. I don't think so.'

'Yet you married him.'

'I was twenty-eight. I was sickened by all the attempts I'd made.'

'You wanted respectability?'

She did not look offended.

'Tranquillity, at any rate.'

'Did you choose Marton in preference to other men because he was more malleable?'

'Unconsciously perhaps.'

'You already knew that he was practically impotent?'

'Yes. That wasn't what I was looking for.'

'In the early days you were happy with him?'

'That's a big word. We got on quite well together.'

'Because he did what you wanted?'

She pretended not to notice either the aggressive note vibrating in the chief-inspector's voice, or the way in which he was looking at her.

'I didn't ask myself that question.'

Nothing put her off her stride, and yet she was beginning to show a certain weariness.

'When you met Harris, or, if you prefer, Maurice Schwob, did you love him?'

She pondered, with a kind of honesty, as if she were determined to be precise.

'You keep on using that word. To begin with, Maurice was able to change my position, and I never considered that I belonged behind a counter in a big store.'

'Did he become your lover straight away?'

'That depends on what you mean by straight away. A few days, if I remember correctly. We neither of us attached any importance to it.'

'Your relations were established rather on a business footing?'

172

'If you like. I know that of two hypotheses you'll choose the dirtier. I'd prefer to say that Maurice and I felt that we were the same sort of people . . .'

'Because you had the same ambitions. You never thought of getting a divorce to marry him?'

'What good would that have done? He's married, to a woman older than himself, who has a private fortune and thanks to whom he's been able to start the Rue Saint-Honoré business. As for the rest . . .'

She implied that the rest was so very unimportant!

'When did you begin to suspect that your husband's mind was unbalanced? Because that was the impression you had, wasn't it?'

'It wasn't an impression. It was a conviction. From the start, I knew that he wasn't quite like other people. He had periods of exaltation, during which he spoke of his work as a man of genius would, and others in which he complained that he was just a failure everybody laughed at.'

'Including yourself.'

'Of course. I understand that it's always like that. During these latter periods, he was gloomy and nervous, watching me suspiciously and then, suddenly, just when I least expected it, launching out into recriminations. At other times, on the contrary, he indulged in insinuations.'

'This didn't make you want to leave him?'

'I think I felt sorry for him. He was unhappy.

When my sister arrived from the States, in deep mourning, playing the inconsolable widow, he began by sulking in her company. She upset his routine and he couldn't forgive her for that. He'd go whole days without saying a word to her.

'I still wonder how she managed it. What did it, no doubt, was her putting on a helpless act.

'That way, he finally had somebody available who was weaker than himself. At least, that was what he thought. You understand? With my sister, he had the impression of being a man, a stalwart, superior creature. . . .'

'You still didn't think of getting a divorce so as to leave him a clear field?'

'They'd have been unhappy together anyway, because my sister, in actual fact, isn't made of putty. On the contrary.'

'You hate her?'

'We've never liked each other.'

'Why, in that case, did you take her under your roof?'

'Because she forced herself on us.'

If Maigret felt a weight on his shoulders, and something like a bad taste in his mouth, it was because he felt that this was all true.

Life, in the cottage in the Avenue de Châtillon, had indeed been lived in the atmosphere which Madame Marton described in a few phrases, and he could imagine the virtually silent evenings in the course of which each person remained wrapped in his hatred.

'What were you hoping for? That it wouldn't last much longer?'

'I went to see a doctor.'

'Steiner?'

'No. Another one. I told him everything.'

'He didn't advise you to try to have your husband certified?'

'He advised me to wait, telling me that the symptoms weren't clear enough yet, that a more violent crisis would occur before long . . .'

'So that you expected this crisis and you were on your guard?'

She gave an imperceptible shrug of the shoulders.

'Have I answered all your questions?' she asked after a silence.

Maigret hunted in his mind, but could not think of anything else he could ask her, for there were scarcely any obscure points left.

'When you stopped on the stairs and saw your husband on the floor, you weren't tempted to go to his help?'

'I couldn't be sure that he hadn't enough strength left to grab the revolver . . .'

'You are convinced that your sister knew about everything you've just told me?'

She looked at him without answering.

What was the good of going on? He would have liked to make her contradict herself. He would have liked to charge her. She gave him no hold over her. She did not shy away either.

'I suppose,' he murmured, throwing a final

shaft, 'you never had any intention of getting rid of your husband?'

'By killing him?'

She made a clear distinction between killing and putting away. When he said yes, she stated simply:

'If I'd found it necessary to kill him, I wouldn't have left anything to chance and I wouldn't be here now.'

This too was true. If anyone was capable of committing a perfect crime, it was this woman.

Unfortunately, she had not killed Marton, and, after relighting his pipe and giving her a malevolent look, Maigret slowly got up, his body and mind both feeling numb, and made for the door to the inspectors' office.

'Get me No. 17, Avenue de Châtillon . . . The concierge's lodge . . . Janvier is in the cottage, at the back of the courtyard . . . I'd like to speak to him on the telephone . . .'

He came back to his place and, while he waited, she put a little powder on her face, as she would have done at the theatre during the interval. Finally the telephone rang.

'Janvier? . . . I'd like you to go to the cottage, without hanging up, and have a good look at a tray, which ought to be in the kitchen . . .'

He turned towards Gisèle Marton.

'A round tray or a square tray?'

'An oblong tray, in wood.'

'An oblong wooden tray, big enough to take three cups and saucers . . . What I want to know is whether there's a mark, a scratch, any sort of sign which makes it possible to tell if the tray has been put one way or another . . . You see what I mean? . . . Just a moment . . . Are the experts still there? . . . Good! Ask them to have a look at a bottle in the broom-cupboard which contains some white powder . . . and test it for finger-prints . . .'

Janvier was able to answer the second question straight away.

'There aren't any prints. They've already examined it. The bottle has been wiped with a wet, rather greasy rag, probably a dishcloth.'

'Has the Parquet arrived?'

'Yes. The examining magistrate isn't pleased.'

'Because I didn't wait for him?'

'More particularly because you took the two women away.'

'Tell him that, by the time he gets to his chambers, it will probably be all over. Which magistrate is it?'

'Coméliau.'

The two men could not stand each other.

'Go and have a quick look at the tray. I'll hold the line.'

He heard the voice of Gisèle Marton, to whom he was no longer paying any attention.

'If you had asked me, I would have told you what you want to know. There is a mark. It wasn't made on purpose. It's the varnish which has formed a blister, on one of the short sides of the oblong.'

Sure enough, a few moments later, Janvier, a little out of breath, told him:

'There's a blister in the varnish.'

'Thank you. Nothing else?'

'In Marton's pocket, they've found a bit of crumpled paper which had contained some zinc phosphide.'

'I know.'

Not that the paper would be in the dead man's pocket, but that they would find it somewhere in the room.

He hung up.

'When you saw your husband go into the kitchen, you suspected what he was going to do, didn't you? That was why you changed the cups round?'

'I changed them round whenever I had the chance.'

'He sometimes changed them round too?'

'That's correct. Only, last night, he wasn't able to, because I didn't let the tray out of my sight.'

At the Boulevard Richard-Lenoir too, there was a tray, not in wood, but in electroplate, which was a wedding present. Maigret's cup and his wife's were the same, except that the chief-inspector's had a scarcely visible crack in it.

Now, they never made a mistake. When Madame Maigret put the tray on the pedestal table, by her husband's armchair, he knew for certain that his cup was on his side, within his reach.

He had got up once more. Madame Marton followed him with her eyes, curious but not afraid.

'Will you come here a minute, Lucas? Find an empty office, never mind which, and go there with her. Stay there until I call you. On your way, tell them to bring me the sister-in-law.'

Madame Marton followed Lucas without putting a single question to the chief-inspector. The latter, once he was on his own, opened his cupboard, took the bottle of cognac that he kept there, not so much for himself as for certain of his customers who sometimes needed it, and poured a spot into the water-tumbler.

When somebody knocked, he shut the cupboard door and just had time to wipe his lips.

'Come in!'

Jenny was shown in, wearing the wan, swollen face, streaked with red, of someone who has been crying.

'Sit down.'

The chair her sister had been sitting in was still warm. Jenny looked around her, puzzled to find herself alone with the chief-inspector.

He remained on his feet, walking round in a circle, not knowing how to tackle her, and finally, planting himself in front of her, said:

'Which lawyer do you want?'

She raised her head sharply, her eyes wide open and moist. Her lips moved, but she did not manage to say anything.

'I would prefer to question you in the presence of your lawyer, so that you don't get the impression that I'm catching you off your guard.'

With tears running down her cheeks, she ended up by stammering:

'I don't know any lawyers.'

He took a Bar year-book from the shelves of the book-case and held it out to her.

'Choose from this list.'

She shook her head.

'What's the use?'

He would so much have preferred it to be the other one!

'You confess?'

She nodded, looked for her handkerchief in her handbag, and unaffectedly blew her nose, so that it became redder than ever.

'You admit that you intended to poison your sister?'

At that, she burst out sobbing.

'I don't know any more . . . Don't torture me . . . I want to get it over quickly. . . .'

Great sobs shook her. She did not think of hiding her wet face.

'You were in love with your brother-in-law?'

'I don't know. I don't know any more. I suppose so . . .'

Her eyes looked at him beseechingly.

'Make it quick, Inspector! . . . I can't stand it any longer. . . .'

And, now that he knew, he took the shortest cuts. Sometimes, as he went past her, he even touched the young woman's shoulders with his hand, as if he understood that she needed some human contact.

'You realized that Xavier wasn't like other people?'

She nodded. She shook her head. She was wrestling with problems that were too complicated for her, and finally she cried:

'It was she who didn't understand him and was driving him mad . . .'

'On purpose?'

'I don't know. He needed . . .'

The words were having trouble in coming.

'I tried . . .'

'To reassure him?'

'You can't imagine the sort of atmosphere we were living in . . . It was only when we were alone, he and I . . . Because, with me, he felt well and confident . . .'

'When he joined you on the embankment, yesterday evening, did he tell you that he was to come here for an examination this morning?'

Surprised that Maigret knew all about it, she gaped at him for a moment.

'Answer me . . . I'm trying, for my part, to set you free as soon as possible . . .'

This she understood. She did not think that the chief-inspector was talking of letting her go, but rather of setting her free from herself, as it were.

'He told me,' she admitted reluctantly.

'Did that frighten him?'

She said yes, with a sniff, and added, once more on the brink of tears:

'He fancied she had won . . .'

Her choice of words revealed the disorder of her thoughts.

'Because it was she who drove him to all that . . . She'd foreseen that he would find the poison, that he would get ideas into his head . . .'

'He hated her?'

She stared at him apprehensively, without daring to reply.

'And you too, you began to hate your sister, didn't you?'

She shook her head. That meant neither yes nor no. She was trying rather to chase away the nightmare.

'Yesterday evening, leaving here,' continued Maigret, 'Marton fancied that after the medical examination he wouldn't be allowed to go free again . . . So he had only one evening left . . . It was his last chance . . .'

The behaviour of the toy salesman might appear incoherent, but none the less it followed a certain logical pattern, and Maigret began to understand certain passages in the treatise on psychiatry. Only, what the author of the book set out in difficult terms and complicated phrases was, in fact, nothing but human nature.

'When he came into the kitchen while you were there . . .'

She shivered, wishing she could stop him talking.

'The tea was already in the cups?'

He was sure of it, and did not need an answer.

'You didn't see him put the powder in?'

'I'd got my back to him. He opened the cutlery drawer and took out a knife. I heard the noise the knives made . . .'

'And you thought he hadn't the courage to put the poison in?'

Maigret recalled the knife, with its dark wooden handle, lying beside the radio which had a catalogue on top of it.

Under the chief-inspector's stern gaze, Jenny struggled a little longer before groaning:

'I felt sorry . . .'

He could have retorted:

'Not for your sister, at any rate!'

And she went on:

'I was sure that he was going to be put away, that Gisèle had won the game . . . So . . .'

'So you took the bottle of phosphide and you poured a good dose into your sister's cup. You had the presence of mind to wipe the bottle.'

'I'd got a wet towel in my hand.'

'You made sure that the cup meant for your sister was on the right side of the tray.'

'Please, Inspector! . . . If you knew what a night I'd had . . .'

'You heard everything?'

How could she have failed to hear?

'And you didn't go downstairs?'

'I was too frightened.'

She trembled at the memory and it was for her sake that he went and opened the cupboard again.

'Drink this.'

She obeyed, choked, and nearly brought up the cognac which was burning her throat.

It was obvious that she had reached the point where she wanted to lie down on the floor and stay still and not hear anything more.

'If only your brother-in-law had told you everything . . .'

Huddled up small, she wondered what she was going to hear now.

And Maigret, remembering things that Marton had said in this very office, explained:

'It wasn't poison that he meant to use to get rid of his wife or to take his revenge on her, but his revolver.'

Hadn't he very nearly brought it off? Don't psychiatrists speak of the strict logic of certain lunatics?

It was in his own cup that he had poured some phosphide while rattling the knives, so quickly that his sister-in-law, who had her back to him, had imagined that he had lost his nerve at the last moment.

He had calculated the dose so as to be ill enough to justify the action he was going to take later, but not enough to die. It was not for nothing that, for months past, he had been haunting public libraries, immersing himself in medical and chemical treatises.

It was Gisèle Marton, by changing the cups round on the tray, who had had this dose, and it had done no more than upset her.

Hadn't Jenny understood all this, during the interminable night she had spent in her room, listening to the noises in the house?

The proof that she understood it now was that she slumped further down in her chair, hanging her head, and that she stammered as if she no longer had the strength to form her words properly:

'It was I who killed him . . .'

He left her to her grief, trying not to make any noise, only afraid of seeing her fall to the floor, then finally, on tip-toe, he went into the inspectors' office.

'Take her downstairs . . . Gently . . . To the infirmary first,' he said.

He preferred to have nothing to do with it. Standing in front of the window, he did not even bother to see which inspectors were making for his office.

It was not his fault. He could not, straight after Marton's first visit, have taken him to the psychiatrist. And the latter, no doubt, would not have taken on the responsibility of certifying him.

There exists, between responsibility and irresponsibility, an indefinite zone, a realm of shadows into which it is dangerous to venture.

Two people, at least, had struggled about in it, while a third . . .

'What shall we do with the other one, Chief?'

He gave a start, turned round, and looked at

the vast inspectors' office like a man who has come back from afar.

'Let her go.'

He had nearly said:

'Chuck her out.'

He waited till his own office was free. Then he went back there and, finding traces of foreign smells lingering in the air, opened the window.

He was taking deep breaths of the damp air when Lucas said behind him:

'I don't know if I've done right. Before going, Madame Marton asked me for permission to make a phone call. I said yes, thinking that it might tell us something.'

'What did she say to him?'

'You know who she spoke to?'

'Harris.'

'She calls him Maurice. She apologized for not being there to open the shop. She didn't give any details. She just said:

' "I'll explain everything to you directly . . ." '

Maigret shut the window, turning his back to it, and Lucas, looking at him, asked uneasily:

'What's the matter, Chief?'

'Nothing. What should be the matter? She said it and she isn't the sort of woman who's wrong. Just now, she's in a taxi, holding a little mirror in front of her nose and repairing her make-up. . . .'

He knocked his pipe out in the ash-tray.

'Ring up the Parquet and, if Coméliau is back, tell him I'm coming over to see him straight away.'

For him, it was all over. The rest was the judges' concern, and he had no desire to be in their place.

Noland, 16 December, 1957